LUCY

THE DIMARCO SERIES

JENNIFER HANKS

LUCY
The Dimarco Series

Copyright © 2016 by Jennifer Hanks
ALL RIGHTS RESERVED

Published by Megaohm Productions LLC
ISBN-13: 978-1-540347-37-4
ISBN-10: 1-540347-37-0

Cover Art by CT Cover Design
Interior Formatting by Author E.M.S.

Published in the United States of America.

This book is dedicated to my sister.
Thank you for having faith in me when I didn't.

Acknowledgments

First and foremost I would like to thank my family. Without their support and encouragement I would've never had the courage to complete "Lucy." Your patience and love were constant reminders of the true meaning of "family."

I would like to send a very special thank-you to JB Salsbury who was never too busy to answer a few questions for me. And by few, I actually mean a lot! Your encouragement always seemed to come at a time when I needed it the most and your insights into the writing world have been invaluable.

Thank you so much to my beta readers, Theresa Wegand, Deborah Brown, and Kylie Sharp! You were tasked with the job of reading a very rough draft from a very new author and were unbelievably kind and encouraging. An extra thank you to Kylie, who not only read for me, but has been my advisor in all things social media! Your generosity with not only your ideas, but also your time means more to me than I can express.

A huge thank you goes out to my editor Judy Brown! Her advice and patience during the entire editing process was priceless to me. I only wish I had thought to have you edit this too! You somehow took my anxiety and turned it into excitement with your constant reassurance and kind words. I hope we have many, many more books to work through together!

Thank you to Amanda Simpson at Pixel Mischief Design! You

were incredibly patient while I sorted through titles and ideas and made a beautiful cover conveying exactly what I wanted for "Lucy." Your talent is remarkable.

I would like to thank two wonderful editors who were unable to edit for me because of their already full schedule, but still kept in contact with me to provide advice and support. Thank you Marion Archer and Vanessa Bridges! I cannot tell you how much your encouragement has meant to me.

My biggest thank you goes out to all of the readers who took a chance on a new author. I've learned so much while I was writing, but I never realized how much of myself would go into my writing. Just knowing that somebody read and enjoyed my work means everything.

And finally, thank you to every author for writing your first book and giving us the courage to write ours. It's a community I'm proud to be a part of.

Prologue

Lucy

"Please!" His blue eyes pleaded while he held on to my hands.

"No." I shook my head. "Absolutely not."

"Why not?"

"Seriously, Ben?" I shook my hands free from his and crossed my arms over my chest. "Why not? Okay. Let me see if I understand what you are asking. You want me to go home with you, pretend to be your girlfriend to your entire family, and go to your brother's wedding?" My voice dripped with sarcasm.

"Yep. That's exactly right."

We were standing outside the arts building on campus where we'd just finished class, and I lowered my voice when I saw a few students curiously look our way.

"Why? And I want the truth." I added when I saw the look on his face.

He sighed, grabbed my hand, and pulled me down beside him on a bench. "Okay. Truthfully?" He squeezed my hand. "My mom goes crazy at weddings. She'll make it her mission to have all of us married or at least dating someone. And if we're not?" He paused and lifted his eyebrow. "She'll try to help."

I couldn't help it when I started to laugh.

1

"Are you seriously laughing at my pain?" He grinned. "This is important."

I snorted in a very unladylike manner. "You need a girlfriend for the weekend so your mom won't figure out you're a man whore?"

"Yes, exactly. I don't want to disappoint my mom. I'm her favorite."

That made me laugh even harder because from the stories he's told me about him and his brothers, there couldn't possibly be a favorite. The poor woman had to be exhausted by all of them.

I smirked. "I think Grace is probably her favorite."

"Why? Because she's the only girl?" He snorted, shaking his head.

"Uh, yeah, that's exactly why. Plus, she's the baby. Your mom waited through seven boys to get Grace. She never gave up on having a girl." My eyebrows drew together. "Does that really not tell you anything?"

He looked shocked. "Shit! I never thought about it like that." He paused. "Okay, then I'm the favorite of the boys."

I just stared at him, shaking my head. He was so oblivious to anything that didn't involve his next hookup or school. For all of his partying and whoring around, it had always surprised me how seriously he took school. I'd asked him one time about his goals, and he'd said it was important to him to do well, to make something of himself. I secretly always thought it was because his dad would kick his ass otherwise. Ben's stories had painted their father as very strict about certain things, especially school.

"Why take me home? Aren't they going to be a little suspicious when I'm not like the other girls you date?"

"I don't date. Plus, I've never taken a girl home. At least not since high school." He stopped and looked at me very seriously. "It's just for the weekend, and it's not until Memorial Day weekend, which is still almost a month away, so we'll already be done with school. Come on, don't you think you'll need a break after finals next week?"

I squinted, silently cursing myself for forgetting my sunglasses, and looked down at my feet. I would need a break after the semester I'd just survived, especially considering it was my final semester. I couldn't believe I was about to graduate with a Master's in Social Work.

"Yeah, I guess a break would be nice." I looked up at Ben and frowned. "But I'm not sure this is a good idea."

He squeezed my hand. "Please, Luce. I promise it'll be fun. Plus, I'll really owe you if you help me out."

I pulled my hand from his and stood. Looking down at him, I sighed. "I need to go. I'm meeting my study group at the library." When I turned to walk away, he yelled, "So you'll do it then?"

I stopped, but I didn't turn around and reluctantly called back. "Yeah, I'll do it."

Shaking my head, I kept walking, but I heard him hoot and laugh.

I was such an idiot.

Chapter One

Lucy

"This was so stupid," I muttered to myself while I was packing. I should've refused, but I hadn't been able to tell Ben no since the day I met him two years ago in an English Lit class. Professor Harkins had pulled me aside one day after class and asked if I would consider tutoring a student who was struggling with the class and assignments. I told him I couldn't because my course load was so full, but Ben found out who Harkins asked and tracked me down himself. That was the day my inability to say no started. In all honesty, it wasn't a hardship to tutor Ben. He was fun to be around, and together, we completed assignments much faster, so it didn't affect my schedule too much. My goal had always been to graduate early, which I had now accomplished, so a weekend away was well earned. Plus, I decided to put in a few job applications while I was there.

When I first moved to North Carolina to attend NC State, I never dreamed my life would have involved someone like Ben. I was always a quiet and serious student, not wanting to be noticed and never really feeling comfortable in groups of people. I never knew what to say or how to act. I learned early on that if I kept to myself, I could avoid the embarrassment of rejection and the anxiety that came with being uncomfortable. I felt comfortable with Ben, though because he reminded me of my brother, Landon.

I quickly finished packing just as the doorbell rang, and I ran to answer it.

Out of breath, I pulled the door open. "Hey."

"Hey, gorgeous." Ben walked through the door and into my living room.

The apartment was so small there wasn't anywhere else to go. We always joked that we only had enough room to turn around in any of the rooms. Not all that funny considering how true it was, but I'd never cared because I liked my little place.

"Stop calling me that," I complained.

"Why?"

"Because people might think we're actually a couple, and they'll tell me how many girls they see you out with when I'm not around," I pointed out.

"You know I don't care what people think. Besides, that's perfect for this weekend, so maybe I'll keep doing it through until Monday, at least." He winked and smirked.

"Whatever." I rolled my eyes. "Okay, you ready?"

He nodded and grabbed my suitcase while I locked up. "So, the drive to my folks is only about three hours." He put my suitcase in the back seat of his truck and jumped in the driver's seat.

"You know, I've been thinking—" I started.

"Oh, shit," he muttered under his breath.

"I heard that." I looked sideways at him with what was supposed to be a stern expression, but it only made him laugh.

"Yeah, yeah. Okay, what have you been thinking?"

"We need to firm up some details of our relationship if you want your family to believe we're together. Don't you think?"

"I guess that's probably a good idea, but we need to keep it simple so we don't screw it up. Trust me, my mom can smell a lie a mile away." He glanced my way. "And no offense, but you suck at lying."

"Um, yeah, that doesn't offend me," I replied with a laugh. "Alright, so why don't we keep everything about us the same? Like how we met, and only add that we started dating recently."

"How recently?"

"Hmm… not long. It should be short so it won't be sad when you tell them we broke up. Not like losing a long-term relationship would be."

"Yeah." He paused, and murmured, "That would be sad, I guess."

I looked over at Ben and wondered about his response. Something else was going on with him, something he wasn't ready to share with me, but I had a feeling it involved a girl. His reasons for asking me to take part in this ridiculous charade were too flimsy. We spent the next few minutes chatting about our new relationship and laughing at how ridiculous the idea of Ben and me together was.

"So tell me a little about your family. Stuff I don't know."

"Like what?" He shrugged.

"I don't know. Something useful so it sounds like we have deep, meaningful conversations."

"I thought we were keeping this light?" he reminded me.

"Well, yeah we are, but just give me a heads-up on stuff that could otherwise take me by surprise."

"Okay. Well, we're going to Jax's wedding. He's marrying Kasey, a teacher at the elementary school."

"I already know that." I sighed.

"There's really nothing to tell. They're great. We get along great."

"That can't be true. No family gets along great all the time," I remarked.

"You'll see," he replied smugly. He looked sideways at me and winked. "You're gonna love them." Then he reached over and squeezed my thigh. "Everything will be fine."

I hoped so.

LUCY

When we saw the sign for New Hope, the town where he grew up and his parents still lived, he announced we had only about twenty more minutes to get there.

We stopped at a few places to drop off some job applications that couldn't be submitted online, then continued to his parents' house. I realized when completing these applications that this small town had traditional small-town ideals and values, which meant most people wanted applications brought to them in person. I assumed they wanted to put a face with a name. Ben talked nonstop about his family and sounded so excited the butterflies in my stomach multiplied, which only reinforced that this was a bad idea.

Chapter Two

Lucy

We pulled into the driveway and had barely turned the car off when the front door flew open. A man and a woman charged out onto the porch, waving at us with huge smiles on their faces.

"I can't believe you're finally here!" Ben's mom yelled as she came out the door. At least I assumed it was his mom by the resemblance to him.

"I'm guessing that's your mom and dad?" I laughed.

Ben smirked and looked at me. "Told you I was her favorite."

Throwing open his door, he met his mom at the front of the car and gave her a huge hug and a kiss on the cheek. He gave his dad one of those guy hugs with one arm, back thumping included. I was watching him with his dad, so I didn't notice his mom open my door until she grabbed my arm, which made me squeal in surprise.

She started laughing. "You must be Lucy." She yanked on my arm until I got out of the car and wrapped her arms around me in a hug. Then she pushed me back and grabbed my hands. "Oh my, aren't you a pretty thing." Pulling me by my hand, she led me to his dad. "Look, Jack, this is Lucy. Isn't she pretty?"

I smiled huge and looked sideways at Ben. "I really like your mom," I said, which made all three of them laugh. Ben's dad, Jack, then hugged me almost as tight as his mom had before I said, "It's nice to meet you Mr. and Mrs. Dimarco."

"Oh no, we aren't formal here. Just call us Jack and Anna." She took my hand and led me into the house, only turning back to tell Jack and Ben to get the bags. I grinned at Ben over my shoulder, finally understanding how Anna has managed this huge family.

Pure chaos. That was the only way I could describe the view in front of me when we walked through the front door. The front entrance to their home had a huge foyer leading to an enormous staircase, and it was packed with people, all talking at once. I barely made it through the door when some of them stopped talking and stared at me while elbowing whoever was closest, encouraging them to stop talking and stare at me too. This continued until everyone was staring at me and completely quiet. I smiled a small, hesitant smile and looked at Anna for support.

"Everyone, this is Ben's girlfriend, Lucy," she announced in a proud voice.

After a slight pause, everyone started moving toward me, greeting me in different ways with a hug before passing me to the next person. Anna leaned in toward me. "Both Jack and I come from large families, and nearly everyone arrived today, but thankfully, they aren't staying with us." She sounded relieved. "Most are at the hotel in town through the weekend. We don't have enough room with all of our kiddos staying here too."

Nodding, I continued saying hello to everyone until Ben came through the door, and their attention switched to him. Thank god.

He pushed through everyone just as Anna said, "Come on, you two. I'll take you upstairs to get settled in."

"Your house is amazing, Anna," I commented as we walked up the wide staircase. At the top was a landing and then a long wide hallway with doors on both sides.

"Oh, thank you, honey. It used to be an old farmhouse until Jack and his brothers fixed it up when the boys were small. They, of course, tried to help too." Anna laughed, obviously stuck in a memory. I turned around to see Ben following me with a grin.

"Jeez, Ma, which room are we getting?" Ben asked.

"Sorry, kiddo, but you're the last ones here, so you get what's left."

"Oh, fuck," he mumbled, and I threw my elbow back and caught him in the stomach.

"Are you seriously using the f-word in front of your mom?" I whispered.

"Don't worry, honey. Raising seven boys, I've heard it all," Anna called out from up ahead of us. "Okay, here we are. I assumed you'd be fine with sharing." She winked at me while she opened the door and then turned to walk in.

"Ma, seriously. Can't someone else who is here alone take this room?"

"What's wrong with this room?" I took a quick look around, and it seemed fine to me.

"All of the other rooms have queen beds. This one only has a double." He shook his head, but then he perked up. "Hey, what about Brody? I know he wasn't planning on bringing anyone."

"Sorry, Ben. You get what you get. If one of the boys will switch with you, that's between you guys." She then looked at me. "Ben's habitually late, but you probably already know that. The trouble is, his brothers know it too, so they always make sure they arrive a little early to pick what they want." She shrugged her shoulders and started to back out the door. "The rehearsal dinner is at six o'clock tonight." Then she pointed her finger at Ben and warned, "Do not be late for that, Benjamin," and closed the door.

I looked at Ben with wide eyes. "You're already in trouble, and we just got here."

He smirked. "I've always been trouble, baby."

I rolled my eyes, making him laugh.

"Sorry about the small bed." He frowned.

"It doesn't bother me," I replied. "I am a little surprised that your mom's okay with us sharing, though, and the wink threw me a little."

He nodded his head in agreement, and we started unpacking. "Yeah, that was kind of strange, but she's probably out of room with all of us here. There really isn't a normal for this situation. None of us ever bring girls home. Especially not for an entire weekend."

The arguing began soon after over important things like what side of the bed was his and how much closet space was mine.

"You're like an annoying little brother," I said, still laughing.

"I'm older than you, so that can't be right."

"You're older by three months." I snorted. "And besides, that's not mental and emotional age. If we consider those, you'd still be a toddler." I laughed harder, appreciating my own humor.

I looked up when I didn't hear him laughing and backed up when I saw him start toward me. Damn, he didn't take that joke well if the look on his face was any indication. I quickly assessed the smartest route to the door to escape, gave one more look his way, and took off. He caught me halfway there and wrapped his arm around my waist, easily throwing me on the bed. I landed with a thump. Jeez, how did he do that? I had no time to react before he was beside me, and he started the dreaded tickling.

I hated being tickled and squealed while laughing. "Ben, stop."

"Take it back," he demanded.

"I ca…can't." I laughed harder.

"Then I can't stop until you do." He paused. "Unless you say I'm the sexiest man you know."

When I hesitated, he paused. "Wait, stop for a minute. Please." Surprisingly, he listened, but his hands stayed in position to torture again. "Okay, you're the sexiest man I know."

"And…" he prompted.

"And what? You said that's all I had to say," I pointed out.

"You rolled your eyes, so now you have to take back the toddler comment too."

I narrowed my eyes and gave him my best annoyed expression before I relented and exclaimed, "Fine! You're not a toddler!"

He stared at me for a minute as if he was trying to determine my sincerity and then rolled to his back to sit up, eyes still on me, when I stupidly mumbled, "More like a big baby."

"I heard that!" he yelled before he pounced again.

"Ben, stop!" I cried out. "I have to pee."

"Ha, I'm going to make you pee on the bed," he said while laughing. "Who's the toddler now?"

"Ben, get the fuck off that girl."

Still laughing to the point there were tears running out of the corner of my eyes, I turned toward the voice and saw a man who was definitely one of his brothers. No doubt. I wasn't exactly lying when I said Ben was the sexiest man I knew, but this guy was also easily in the running for that particular title.

Ben paused. "Hey, Luke."

Ah, so this was Luke. Yummy.

"Listen, this is the least she deserves." His expression became serious. "She called me a toddler and," he paused, rolled his lips together and shook his head all before saying very seriously, "she questioned my sexiness."

I smiled at Luke and shrugged my shoulders as best I could while still lying down.

Before he could respond, another ridiculously good-looking male chewing on something appeared behind Luke.

"What's going on?" He shoved the last bit of whatever he was holding into his mouth.

"She called him a toddler," Luke answered dryly, moving into the room and crossing his arms over his chest.

"And questioned my sexiness!" Ben jokingly complained while the other man came the whole way in and stood right where my feet were hanging off the bed.

"Hi. I'm Jake. This idiot's brother." He continued chewing and motioned toward Ben.

"I'm Lucy. It's nice to meet you." When he smiled, I decided to go for it. "Could you please get him off me?"

Jake watched me thoughtfully. "Did you really question his sexiness and call him a toddler?"

I looked at Ben, who was smirking at me and narrowed my eyes. Taking a deep breath, I looked back at Jake and mumbled, "Yes."

"Then, fuck yeah, I'll help you!" he yelled.

Wait, what? Then Jake's big body flew over top of mine and tackled Ben beside me. Having no way to escape, I ended up between the two of them, trying to shimmy off the bed.

"Stupid, fucking idiots." I heard someone say, then felt someone pulling on my feet while the two wrestling bodies were pulled apart. I had my arms over my face and around my head when I felt my butt clear the end of the bed and an arm circled my waist to pull me up against a hard body. A hand was on the back of my head pushed my face into a chest. "What the hell is wrong with you two?"

"You okay?" Soft words were whispered by my ear.

His warm breath floated across my ear, and I shivered. What was that? With my hands lying against his chest, I could feel the outline of muscle through his navy-blue Henley. Slowly, I let my eyes wander up over his wide chest and thick neck until I was looking into deep blue eyes, the same color as Ben's, but the face was different. Where Ben was soft and boyish, this guy was rough and masculine. His jawline cut a little sharper, his cheekbones a little higher, but even with those differences, there was no doubt this was Ben's brother. With dark hair a little long on top and stubble giving an "I don't care" sexy vibe on his jaw, he was walking and talking sex. My breath hitched when he ran his hand up along my side and over my shoulder until he rested it on the side of my face, holding my cheek. He was looking at me expectantly, obviously waiting for my answer to the question I'd forgotten he asked.

Realizing I was staring, I shook my head and cleared my throat. "Uh, yeah, fine. I'm fine," I stammered. "Thank you."

I pushed away and turned around to see Ben and Jake staring at me with sheepish looks on their faces.

Ben stepped forward first. "Sorry, Luce. You okay?"

"Yeah, I'm fine. No harm done." Laughing, I looked at Jake. "Thanks for your help?" But it sounded like a question.

The guys laughed, and Ben turned to the one who'd saved me. "Chris, man, this is Lucy."

I looked behind me and up to see him looking down at me, and I swallowed. His eyes narrowed a little, and he tilted his head to the side. I smiled but felt my face getting hot while his eyes slowly wandered over me. It was as if time stopped, and for one moment, he and I were the only ones in the room. Looking into his eyes, I felt as if I'd known him forever. Jeez, what was it about this brother?

"Lucy. As in your girlfriend?" Chris asked, finally looking toward Ben and breaking the spell I'd been under.

I moved to stand beside Ben and wished immediately that I had stayed next to Chris, already missing the connection.

"Yeah, man." He faced me. "Luce, this is another brother, Christian. Everyone calls him Chris."

"The twin?" I asked excitedly, still looking at Christian, who finally looked back down at me with a strange hardness in his eyes.

"Yeah, Cam's my twin," he answered.

"He's deployed, right?" When a strange silence came over the room, I looked at Ben.

He gave me a soft smile. "Yeah Luce, but everyone's a little worried. We haven't heard from him in a while."

I glanced at Christian again. "Oh, I'm so sorry. I didn't know."

When no one said anything, I tried one more time in my perkiest voice, "Well, no news is good news, right?" Okay, still nothing. Feeling awkward, I looked down at the floor and wished I would have kept my thoughts to myself when Ben put his hand on my shoulder. I glanced up and saw a look of remorse pass through his eyes.

"Alright, let's get out of here. Let these two do whatever the hell they were doing," Luke said, bringing my attention back to him. He turned to walk out the door but not before he smiled and winked at me. I smiled shyly at Jake and Christian as they walked by me. Jake gave me a shoulder pat, but I noticed that Christian did everything he could to avoid my eyes.

Once the door closed, I looked at Ben with wide eyes. "Jeez, Ben. You could have told me about Cam."

"I'm sorry." He looked at me sadly. "Nobody likes to talk about it, myself included, and especially not Chris."

"I feel really bad. Should I apologize again or something?" I asked, sincerely.

"Nah, it's best if you leave it alone. Okay?"

"Yeah, okay." I bit down on my lip, but then released it. It was a horrible nervous habit of mine that I couldn't seem to break.

Ben announced he was going to hang out with his brothers for a little while, and I decided to take a shower and change so I could hopefully help Anna. I definitely would feel better helping rather than just standing around.

Ben showed me where one of the two bathrooms on the second floor were and left me on my own. I stood in front of the mirror after my shower and stared at my face. I'd always considered myself average, but in this house of beautiful people, I was feeling below average. I definitely needed to put on my armor. I started with some makeup, enough to show I made an effort but not enough to look like I was going clubbing with the girls. Not that I'd ever done that. I concentrated on my eyes because they were probably my best feature in a pretty shade of green. I paused while putting on mascara and realized that even though this was fake with Ben, I didn't want to embarrass him. My hair was a different story because it was naturally curly and dark blond. I'd thought about dying it to be a lighter blond, but it always sounded like too much upkeep, so I'd left it natural. I put in some product to keep the curl from becoming a ball of frizz and blow-dried it a little. It's all one length, which has kept styling it fairly simple.

After I was done, I peeked out into the hallway to see if I was alone. I was feeling a little uncomfortable only being in my robe and wished I had thought to bring my clothes in with me instead. The coast seemed clear, so I made a mad dash for our room and quickly shut the door, realizing if anyone saw that, they were probably laughing their ass off.

I had brought two dresses with me, one fancier than the other so I wouldn't have a hard time deciding once I was here. My dress for tonight was a black sundress that tied around my neck and had little pink and yellow flowers on it. I also grabbed the pink sweater I brought along in case I got cold and put on my shiny black pumps with a three-inch heel that tied around my ankle. I loved those shoes. Absolutely nothing was special about them except they made me feel sexy. I liked to wear them when I felt a little out of my comfort zone.

I was suddenly glad I'd brought them here.

Walking to the mirror that hung on the back of the door, I did a full body check. Hips, ass, and boobs. That was all I saw. No amount of exercise had ever changed the hips or ass. I was okay with the boobs. I didn't get it, though, my twin brother had no hips or ass. I must have taken it all in utero. Lucky bastard.

Walking down the stairs, I found myself admiring the simplicity of their house. Regardless of its size, it felt warm and cozy and like a home, not merely a house. I could feel all the laughter and warmth surrounding me like a blanket. I found Anna downstairs in the kitchen with the catering staff and stood back for a while watching her boss everyone around and chuckling to myself before she noticed me.

"Lucy." She walked over and grabbed my hand. "You look lovely, honey."

"Thank you." I smiled, and then hesitantly asked, "Is this okay? I wasn't sure how dressy this dinner would be."

"Oh, absolutely. It's perfect." She smiled widely. I took the time to look at her and noticed she was wearing a very pretty but simple pantsuit.

"You look really nice too." I said.

"Thank you, dear."

"Can I help with something?"

"Oh, well I don't think so." She looked around. "I decided to have it catered so we wouldn't have to do all the work." She turned back toward me and snapped her fingers, "You could do me one favor if you wouldn't mind."

"Sure. What do you need?"

"I finished up the flower arrangements for the centerpieces on the tables, but I haven't had time to set them up. Would you mind doing that?"

"Sure. I can do that." I smiled, glad to have something to do. "Just show me where they are."

She gave me a relieved smile, and we walked outside to where the flowers were waiting on a long table by the door. I took a minute to look around their beautiful yard decorated with white tables and chairs. White china on buttercup yellow linen, and huge bunches of daisies with baby's breath arranged throughout them, adorned the tables. Very simple but beautiful. The yard was massive, and at the bottom end was an enormous swimming pool surrounded by elaborate landscaping and a fountain. I looked down when I heard the *click clack* of my heels and realized someone had taken the time to lay pavers along the grass, creating a walkway for girls wearing high heels. Everyone knew trying to walk through grass in heels was a nightmare. Was there anything they hadn't thought of?

I carried the arrangements to the tables, thirty in all. I'd just put the fifth one on when I heard someone say behind me, "Here's two more."

I turned to see Christian holding two more arrangements with a frown on his face. That frown did nothing to take away from his looks. I noticed he had changed and was wearing dark jeans and a button-down light blue shirt with the sleeves rolled up to his elbows. He looked amazing. He smelled even better, I noticed, when I was lucky enough to catch his scent on the small breeze blowing around us.

"Thanks, but I can finish this on my own," I answered softly while he looked around the yard at anywhere but me.

"Got my orders from the boss herself and not one of us says no to Mom, grown or not," he growled while squinting a little in the bright sun.

He met my eyes, and for the first time since we arrived, and I regretted my decision to come as Ben's girlfriend. I couldn't help but wonder if Christian felt the same attraction as me, but I wasn't brave enough to explore that. I wasn't single either, apparently.

"Oh." I nodded. "Okay then. Well, thanks." I took the two arrangements to add to the tables while he walked away to get more. We worked in silence for the remainder of time it took to place all the centerpieces until we were down to the last two.

He turned to walk away, saying, "Well, that's it."

I couldn't let him leave without saying something. I felt so bad about earlier and knew that was why he was being short with me.

"Christian." I called out before he had gone too far.

He stopped walking, putting his hands on his hips, and I saw his head drop to look at the ground before he turned toward me.

I walked to him, which forced him to look at me. "I am so sorry about earlier." I paused, and when he didn't say anything, I kept going. "Ben said not to say anything more to you, but I feel so bad that I brought up your brother. I swear I didn't know you haven't heard from him." *Okay, stop talking now.* "I just thought it was cool that you have a twin because I do too. We're not identical, though, and mine's a guy, so that's similar I guess," I rambled on, making no sense while he tilted his head to the side, and his eyes widened. "But you're probably closer to yours because of the identical thing. We don't have the twin telepathy thing, but I can't imagine not knowing where he is and how he is." *Stop talking!* "So, yeah." I looked at the ground. "I'm really sorry."

When I looked up again, he was already walking away.

I guess Ben was right after all.

Chapter Three

Lucy

It was entertaining, to say the least, to sit back and watch Ben's family interact with one another at the rehearsal dinner, which appeared to go off without any problems. His brothers teased each other constantly, and I finally met the infamous Grace who was as much adored by her brothers as her parents. I felt bad for her, though. I couldn't imagine bringing home a boyfriend to this family as the only girl and the youngest. It was like she had eight fathers, including her actual father. I was introduced to Kasey and Jax but only said hello because everyone was demanding their time. I also met their one-year-old daughter, Mia, a beautiful combination of her parents.

Before they moved on, Kasey did pull me aside, though, to say it was nice to finally meet another girl dating one of the brothers who wasn't a skank. Her words, not mine, but from what I'd heard, maybe not wrong.

Ben and I behaved as we always did and teased each other all night. It was fun even though my conscience screamed at me that we should feel bad about this. But for the life of me, I couldn't see how we were hurting anyone. I only regretted my decision because of Christian, but he had still not given me any sign he was interested in me as anything more than Ben's friend.

At one point, when dinner was over and Ben was with his brothers, I found myself alone, so I wandered toward the pool. I couldn't even imagine growing up in this place with a family like this. My family was great. My brother, Landon, and I were close growing up and still are. My parents were always a little too busy with their careers, but they did their best for us and loved us in their own way. We simply never had these relationships, but honestly, before I met this family, I would have said people and relationships like these didn't exist.

The property was beautiful and so peaceful. The smell of the flowers near the pool was strong but not overbearing, and they added a sweetness to the already tranquil setting. Because I sometimes needed to be alone, I found a bench near the fountain and decided to sit and watch the celebration from afar. Sitting alone, I was completely immersed in my own thoughts when someone sat down beside me.

"What are you doing down here?" he asked.

I looked up and smiled when I saw it was Jack who had found me. "I think the better question is, what are you doing down here?"

"You looked like you could use some company." He had an innocent look on his face, but I noticed the hint of a smile.

I nodded slowly. "Uh-huh. So who are we hiding from?"

He laughed and shook his head. "That damn brother of Anna's won't leave me alone." He paused. "George. Known the man almost forty years, and he still gets on my nerves. Follows me around. I can't lose him."

I faced forward and considered that for a moment. "Maybe he wants to be like you," I suggested quietly. "You know, all this time trying to learn how you tick so he can emulate you. Sometimes it's tough to be in your own skin. Sometimes it seems it would be better to be like someone else. Someone who's easily loved and appreciated." I looked over and bit down on my lip before releasing it. "I could totally see that."

He smiled softly, and I noticed the crinkles and lines around his mouth and eyes. Laugh lines from a life of great family and fun times. I could see all the boys' different features on his face. His hair was dark brown, like all his children, but threaded with strands of silver that only made him look more distinguished. I also noticed he shared his deep blue eyes with Christian and Ben while the other brothers had a lighter shade of blue. Brody's and Anna's eyes were a different shade of blue, so unique, I was sure I'd never seen the color before. Jack was as handsome as all of them, and I could only imagine what Anna felt when she'd first laid eyes on him.

"Well, shit. Now you've made me feel bad."

I giggled and turned my head forward when he motioned for me to look in front of us. Smiling softly, I watched almost all of his boys walking toward us. What a force they seemed when all together. Strong, intense, and so ridiculously hot, it made me wonder what the hell they put in the water around here.

"Would you look at them." I took a moment to look at Jack and saw the pride shining in his eyes while he watched them. "Those boys are responsible for every gray hair on this head, and you know what?" He paused and looked at me, smiling. "I wouldn't trade it for anything. Best years of my life with those boys." He sighed with a hint of sadness.

"It seems to me like some of the best may still be to come. You know, with marriages and babies." I leaned my shoulder against his. "I'll bet being a grandpa kicks ass."

When he didn't say anything, I lifted my head and looked back over at him. "You're good for him, you know that?" He looked at the boys. "You're exactly what he needs right now."

Wow. Hello, conscience. Before I could say more, the boys approached, and Ben yelled out, "Pop, you flirting with my girl?"

"Couldn't help myself, boy." He smirked at me and put his arm around my shoulders for a quick squeeze. "Alright, I better head back before Anna realizes I'm gone."

"She already knows," Jake said. "She sent us down to tell you Uncle George is looking for you."

They burst out laughing at the same time and made comments meant to tease their dad, but he looked down at me and smiled. Looking back toward the boys, he shrugged. "Of course, he is. Who wouldn't want to spend time with me?" That made me laugh along with the boys while Jack walked back toward the house.

"Come on, Luce. It's a nice night, so we're gonna build a fire." I took the hand Ben held out to me and let him pull me up off the bench. Looking toward his brothers, I saw varying expressions on their faces, including amusement and curiosity. When I settled on Christian's face, I noticed he wasn't looking up, but instead, he seemed to be staring at our hands. I watched him, hoping he would look up so I could smile and maybe break some of this awful tension between us, but he never looked at me. Ben gave my hand a tug, breaking my focus from Christian's downturned face, and we led the way back to the house.

The entertaining stories the boys told about each other around the fire were ridiculously funny. I learned a lot about Ben, including the competitive streak I'd never really seen in him. When I mentioned that, he responded that he'd never had any reason to compete with me. Everyone was talking and laughing, and it seemed even Christian was enjoying himself. Maybe I hadn't screwed up quite as badly as I thought.

Ben left to take a call when the fire started to burn out, and the conversations quieted. It wasn't long until everyone was saying good night, and I realized I was alone with Christian. He sat in the same place he had occupied all evening, right across from me, with the fire burning between us. I'd never realized how intimate it could feel just sitting with another person in the firelight.

I watched as he leaned forward, legs spread, and put his elbows on his knees. With his head hanging between his legs and his hands rubbing the back of his neck, knots began to form in my stomach. I wanted to say something, anything, but with the way our last conversation had gone, I wasn't sure he wanted that, so I sat quietly.

I was thinking I should go look for Ben when I heard, "So, how long have you known Ben?"

I jolted at the sudden break in the silence and raised my eyes from the fire to Christian's. Surprised that he had initiated conversation, I cleared my throat and smiled. "About two years now, I guess."

"How did you meet?" He rubbed his hands together, still sitting with his elbows on his knees.

"I was his English Lit tutor." I was nervous talking to him like this and knew he had to be able to tell, but he didn't let on if he did.

He nodded. God, this was awkward. Clearing my throat again, I asked, "So where do you fall in line with your brothers?" Cocking his head, he stared at me, and I assumed he was confused by what I was asking or rather how I was asking, so I tried again. "I mean, I know Jax is the oldest and Grace is the youngest, but I don't know the rest of the order."

He smiled. Finally, a smile. Okay, I would get him to talk about his family. Well, all except Cameron.

"It's Jax, Luke, Brody, then Cam and I, and then Jake, Ben, and Grace."

"Were you all close growing up?"

"Yeah, I guess we were but in different ways."

I shook my head. "What do you mean?"

"Well, Jax, Luke and Brody were always together. They played together. They were in school together. There's a three-year age difference between Cam and I and Brody, so they always seemed a lot older than us. It wasn't until later in school that we became closer like we are now. Cam and I were always together anyway. We never really included anyone else." He smirked. "That bugged the hell out of Jake and Ben when they were younger. And of course, then Grace came along, and everything changed."

"How did it change?" I felt like I was on borrowed time, and if I asked the wrong thing, he would leave. This was the most he'd talked to me, and I didn't want it to end yet. Not to mention,

I loved his voice. It was deep and rough, not smooth at all. I could have listened to him all night.

He shrugged his shoulders. "We didn't know what to do with a little girl. I don't even think my dad knew what he was doing. I remember feeling protective of something for the first time in my life. I think she changed all of us a little." He smiled softly, and I realized then that I could listen to his stories forever if they put that look on his face. "She didn't play like we did, either. She was all girl, which my mom loved, but we were all boy." Cocking his head as if something just occurred to him, he looked at me curiously. "Hasn't Ben talked about us and growing up?"

Crap. He was right. This was all stuff I should've already known if Ben and I were really in a relationship. The truth was, I did know some of it, but I wanted to hear Christian tell me. Feeling flustered, I said the worst thing I could've said right then. "Ben and I don't talk a lot when we're together."

I realized my mistake when he jerked back, and even through the firelight, I could see the easy expression he had worn was gone. He nodded his head, stood slowly, and started walking away. "I'll send Ben down to put the fire out."

Without thinking, I jumped up and walked quickly until I was right behind him, then grabbed his arm. He turned around, and I was sad to see the warmth was gone from his eyes and the distance was back.

"That wasn't what I meant." I spoke quickly. "I only meant that we don't have that kind of relationship."

He narrowed his eyes and reached out to lay his hand on my hip. "What kind of relationship?"

I swallowed hard, feeling only his hand against me. Moving closer, almost as if there was a magnet pulling me toward him, I curled my hand around the bicep it was already resting against. He moved his hand until it rested against my side, his thumb brushing back and forth over my dress, right below my breast. My breath hitched, watching his head lower toward mine. I could already imagine what his lips would feel like, taste like, and I couldn't remember ever wanting something more than I wanted to feel his lips against mine.

His breath floated across my lips the closer he got. "What kind of relationship, Lucy?" he whispered, looking into my eyes. He looked intense, almost hopeful, and his hand tightened against me.

I realized at that moment that I wanted nothing more than to tell him the truth. To admit that Ben and I were only friends and could only ever be friends. "Christian, I…"

"Lucy." I jumped back at the sound of Ben's voice calling my name. What was I doing? I couldn't do that to Ben. For whatever reason, he needed me to do this, and I needed to keep my promise to him. Christian reached for me, and I backed away, shaking my head.

"I'm sorry," I whispered. Starting across the yard toward Ben who was standing in the open doorway of the house, I looked back to see Christian watching me. Feeling a sadness and loss I couldn't explain, I wrapped my arms around myself and turned back to the brother I had already promised myself to. For this weekend, anyway.

Chapter Four

Lucy

I woke up scrunched on the side of the bed with something heavy lying across my back when the bed moved, and I shifted. What the hell?

"You better not be doing what I think you're doing," I mumbled.

I heard a ton of laughter then and realized we weren't alone. I wasn't looking up. How many were in here, and was there no such thing as privacy?

I buried my face in my pillow and heard Ben say, "Luce, really, what kind of guy do you think I am?"

I felt his arm, which I now realized was the heavy thing across my back, tighten around me, and I groaned. Crap, I had to pee, and there was no way I was getting out of this bed with an audience.

"Baby, something's happening with your hair. I think it grew overnight or something." Ben laughed.

I immediately put my hands on the back of my hair and pushed it down. Seriously, could this get worse? Since my hair was usually crazy in the morning, giving new meaning to the term bedhead, I had a pretty good idea what it looked like. And since when does Ben call me baby? I was putting a stop to that as soon as I got a minute alone with him.

"What the hell are you guys doing?" a deep voice growled.

And it just got worse. I was almost positive that was Christian's voice.

"You know Mom would kick your asses if she knew you were in here bothering Lucy," he warned.

"We're not bothering her, are we Luce?" Who the hell was that? Why do they all have to sound the same?

I turned my head to the side a little so I could breathe and answer the question, never letting go of my hair, though.

"Umm, well, no, of course not." I sighed.

"Lucy doesn't care. She's cool like that," Ben defended himself.

I'll admit I try to be cool. And maybe if I'd known these people a little longer than a day, not been in a fake relationship with their brother, and had normal hair, I would be much cooler. But I was none of these things, and I really wanted to yell, "Get out. I have to pee." I didn't, of course, because I also had a problem with wanting everyone to like me, which was why this stuff with Christian was bothering me so much. I figured that out around two this morning when I still couldn't fall asleep because Ben, I discovered, was a bed hog who slept like the dead, so I couldn't even move him over. I just hung onto the bed for dear life and tried hard not to scream in his face. I barely succeeded.

"Cool or not, this can't be fun for her. And Ben, don't you think you should consider how she feels?" Christian asked.

Ben stiffened beside me. "Fuck you, Chris. Don't think you know Lucy better than I do after one day, man. I've known her for two years, and I know she's fine with this shit, or I would've said something."

He knew nothing. I was not okay. But I didn't want any more tension with Christian because of me, so I did the only thing I could and will live with the embarrassment for the rest of my life. I got out of bed and faced the boys. I immediately placed the voices with the faces and realized thankfully it was only Jake and Luke, along with Christian.

I held my hair back as well as I could and smiled. "Morning, guys."

"Sorry, Lucy." Luke apologized. "We only stopped to talk to Ben for a minute when we saw the door was open, but we should've left."

He leaned in a little with a cocky smirk on his face, "To be honest, though, after the insinuation that he was jerking off, I kind of wanted to stick around and hear what else you had to say."

Laughing, I nodded. "No worries. I don't mind, but I am going to leave now."

I smiled at Jake, who was also smirking, and then took a chance and looked at Christian. I couldn't decipher the look on his face, but he seemed a little mad. He did a scan of me from head to toe as I walked toward him to leave the room. I immediately regretted my choice of pajamas from the night before. The pajama bottoms were okay, but the tank top left little to the imagination, especially considering I had on no bra. Crap.

I tried to go between Jake and Luke to leave, but when I was almost there, Luke moved over closer to Jake so I was forced to go between him and Christian. I did my best to walk out with some dignity, but let's face it, how dignified could I have really been in that situation? When I walked by Christian, my arm brushed against his, and I felt an immediate tingling sensation running down my arm. I didn't stop to look at him or see if he had any reaction to that small touch. Instead, I kept my head down and moved quickly out of the room to the bathroom down the hall.

Once in the bathroom, I closed the door and leaned back against it with my hand to my chest. I let out the breath I didn't realize I'd been holding. What was it about him that I was so attracted to? Maybe because he had defended me in the bedroom twice now when he thought I needed someone. Or maybe because every time he looked at me, my skin felt hot and my heart raced. No matter how small it started, the time I spent with him last night did nothing but intensify it. Rubbing my hand down my arm, I felt a tingle as though he was still touching me, and I realized I needed to squash whatever this was becoming. I could not be attracted to Christian. I needed to focus on getting through today, and then tomorrow, we would leave. I would probably never see Christian again, so there was no use in worrying. Why was it that never seeing him again felt so awful?

After spending enough time in the bathroom to be sure the guys would be gone, I went back to get everything I'd need to shower, making sure to grab my clothes this time to avoid any more potential embarrassment. Once done in the bathroom, I went back to the bedroom to finish getting ready. I figured I would be dressed, and then if anyone needed help, I could pitch in. I looked in the mirror behind the door and surveyed my look. I left my hair down but tamed the curls so it was lying nicely, or as nicely as it could. I did subtle makeup and light lip gloss to add some shine. My dress was green, almost the color of jade, strapless and fitted in the bodice, then loose to my knees. It was comfortable and pretty and the best part was it never wrinkled, so it would look good all day. I put my favorite black pumps on again, added some earrings, and gave myself a quick pep talk about who I was here with before heading downstairs.

Downstairs was in full swing, and I was immediately put to work. Anna explained the wedding ceremony would be held in the church because their Catholic upbringing was important to Jax and Kasey. The reception would be here at the house right after. I looked outside and noticed the catering staff was back and moving about quickly, setting up tables and adding linens again. A band was setting up down near the pool, where a stage and dance floor had been built. When did they do that? It wasn't there last night. As if he read my mind, Jack appeared behind me. "My crew put that in this morning pretty early."

I nodded. "I think I need a crew to do stuff for me."

He chuckled, and I turned to face him. "Wow, you look very handsome," I complimented him. And he did. He was already in his traditional tux, black with black bow tie and black cummerbund.

"E tu sei bella," he replied.

"You speak Italian?" I asked excitedly. I may have even jumped up and down a little, but who could blame me. I had always wanted to learn a foreign language. "What did you say?"

He chuckled and nodded. "Yes, some. My father used to speak in Italian when he upset my mom, so mainly everything I know is compliments. I said, 'And you are beautiful.'"

I couldn't help it when I swooned. I'd never been complimented like that. "Did it work? I mean, with your mom."

He leaned in toward me, looked all around us, and lowered his voice "Every time."

I leaned in too, having no idea why we were acting as if it was a secret between us. "Why are we whispering?"

He looked around again, "Because I do the same thing with Anna, and I don't want her to hear me."

I nodded and smirked, but I had a strong feeling she already knew. Not much seemed to get past Anna.

"Do the boys speak it too?" I asked.

"Speak what?" I turned to see Brody standing behind us and tried to hide my surprise that he was joining the conversation. I'd met him yesterday, but besides saying hello, he had been silent. He seemed broodier than the others and moody. I noticed he stayed silent throughout dinner and spent a lot of time with Jax and Jack. When I asked Ben about him, he told me that Brody and Jax worked together, so they were close. They apparently run a security company or something. Of all the brothers, Brody probably intimidated me the most. Well, maybe second only to Christian.

Jack turned toward him, and answered, "Italian."

Brody looked my way and nodded. "Yeah, we all speak some."

This was so embarrassing. I had no idea what to say to because I found him so intimidating, but I figured no matter what I said to him, it would have sounded ridiculous. Why wasn't Jack talking? They were both just staring at me, and I was choking. Finally, when the silence become too loud, I smiled and nodded.

He smirked, gave me a chin lift, and looked at his dad. "Mom's looking for you."

They kept talking to each other and wandered off to find Anna. Okay. That had been awkward. It was definitely time to find Ben.

Chapter Five

Lucy

The wedding was beautiful, but how could it not be with all the work the family had put into it. Kasey looked like a princess in her dress and had only one friend, Kara, standing with her. Kara wore a light yellow sundress and held Mia, who wore a mini version of Kara's dress, until about halfway through when she got antsy and was handed off to Anna. Both girls carried small bouquets of daisies, and like everything else with this wedding, they were very understated. I was learning that simplicity was a characteristic that Kasey and Anna shared. Brody stood with Jax. Ben explained that because their family was so large and Kasey was an only child, they felt like having only one person stand for each of them was easier. They were all so close, I imagined it was hard on Jax to have only one brother up front with him.

Ben sat with me the whole time as the doting boyfriend except for the few times I caught him checking out some of Kasey's friends, for which he earned an elbow to the stomach. I then got his most charming smile that made most girls fall all over themselves to get to him. I had to admit it did have quite the impact. Jake and his date, Julie, sat on the other side of me. I hadn't figured out their relationship yet, except that it could only be based on sex because her personality was shit. Believe me, I tried, but she

32

was not nice at all. She was like every mean girl I knew in high school who hadn't yet grown up and maybe never would.

Once we were at the reception and dinner was starting, Ben grabbed my arm and pulled me to a table. Our table consisted of us, Jake and Julie, Brody, Grace, Luke, and unfortunately, Christian. Jeez, Brody and Christian at one table. Cue the stupid comments. Luckily, I didn't have to say much because the brothers kept us all entertained with their teasing and observations. Julie complained about everything, and at one point, Grace caught me looking at Julie with what I'm sure was a fairly disgusted look on my face. I quickly tried to make my expression blank, but she'd already caught me, so I simply shrugged my shoulders. With a laugh, she leaned toward me, nodded her head toward Julie, and rolled her eyes. We shared in a private laugh, and I'd decided right then that Grace and I could have definitely been great friends. I mean if I wasn't lying to all of them about Ben and me. I felt really bad when I realized this family was all about honesty and togetherness. I immediately decided it was all Ben's fault, and now he had also cost me a new friendship. I let him know that when I frowned at him while shaking my head. He looked confused and then looked around the table, probably for help, but nobody was looking at us, so he was totally on his own. He avoided my face after that, so my frowning didn't work anymore.

Dinner ended, and everyone started to filter through the crowd, chatting and dancing. Ben and I danced and sang along to the songs we knew. This felt more comfortable. Ben and I spent time out dancing with our friends at school sometimes. When a slow song played, he wanted to keep dancing, so we did. I always liked dancing with Ben because he was so much taller than me, and even with my heels on, I could lay my head on his chest.

I wasn't paying attention to much except how much fun I was having and how comfy I was when I heard Ben say, "Why don't we switch partners for this one?"

Wait, what? I didn't want to switch. When I looked up, I met Christian's eyes. No, no, no. Not Christian.

"What do you say, Luce? Wanna switch?" Ben asked.

What do I say? I say no! I screamed in my head, but I obviously couldn't say that out loud without looking crazy.

"Umm, sure. Why not?"

Ben smiled down at me and then pushed me toward Christian. I finally took a look at who Christian had been dancing with and frowned at Ben. Of course, he wanted to switch. That was the girl he was checking out at the church. He smirked at me and shrugged while he grabbed her around the waist.

That was when I realized that Christian and I were still just standing there, and I smiled at him. "We don't have to dance if you don't want to."

He continued to stare at me, not saying anything, which was making me crazy nervous. I turned to walk away when his arm circled my waist, and he pulled me toward him. He pulled me close, so close I could feel every inch of his body pressed against mine. Like Ben, he was tall, and his body felt especially hard against my softer one. He put both of his hands on my shoulders and ran them down my arms, leaving a trail of goose bumps behind them. He encircled my wrists and pulled my arms up and around his neck, which pulled me even closer, if that was possible, and then moved his arms back around my waist. My head rested on his chest, right above his heart, which was beating loud and fast. I realized we were basically hugging, considering we hadn't started moving yet.

He leaned down, and I felt his mouth at my ear, his breath hot when he whispered, "I want to."

Oh, my god. I actually felt dizzy. I tried to relax my stiff body and slow my breathing, embarrassed because he had to notice. My heart started to beat even faster as he ran one of his hands up my back slowly and into my hair. He gently pushed my head into his chest again where I'd laid it, cheek over his heart, and rested his chin on the top of my head while his hand played with my hair. I was completely surrounded by him like no one else was near us. Like we were in our own perfect bubble that was both safe and intoxicating.

We danced slowly, hardly moving at all. It felt erotic the way he continued to run his hand up my back and into my hair. I breathed deep and relaxed against his warm body. He smelled so good. A little like cologne and lot like a man. I nuzzled my nose into his shirt and inhaled. Oh wow, I wished I could have bottled that smell and carried it around with me.

Using his hand at my waist, he pushed me in closer until I felt him hard and long against my belly. My breath hitched, and I heard him groan softly as I rubbed against his hardness. My stomach roiled in that really delicious way, telling me that if he didn't stop, I was going to need a panty change. I closed my eyes, realizing at that moment that I was ridiculously turned on by him. Ben's brother. My fake boyfriend's brother. That crossed so many lines I couldn't even count them all. When he lowered his head and buried his face in my hair at my neck, inhaling, I conceded to the fact that a panty change was now inevitable.

I had never been this turned on in my life, which wasn't saying much, considering my limited experience, but still this felt unbelievable. I took a moment to look over his shoulder, feeling like we had to be making a scene, but surprisingly, no one was even looking at us.

Unfortunately, and way sooner than I liked, the song ended and a fast one started, effectively breaking the moment. I pulled back quickly at the same time he did. Swallowing hard, I dropped my arms before looking up and meeting his eyes. He shook his head and ran his hand along the back of his neck while staring back at me.

"Thanks," I muttered, but he didn't respond. I jumped a little when Ben came up beside me and swung his arm around my shoulders.

"Thanks, man, but I'm stealing her back now." I glanced at Christian right as Ben turned us around, and we walked away. His eyes were hard and cold, and he held his fists clenched at his sides. What the hell was that?

Chapter Six

Lucy

I woke alone on Sunday morning with a headache and a little bit of a hangover. After the dance with Christian, I decided copious amounts of alcohol were in order. I stuck close to Ben too, only breaking away for more alcohol and to use the bathroom. The happy couple left about halfway through the reception, which I thought was sweet. Ben figured it was because Mia was staying with his parents and they had a night alone. His thinking was probably more accurate. I could only imagine how tough a one-year-old could be on alone time.

I grabbed my phone to check the time and saw that it was ten. Not knowing what time Ben wanted to head home, I decided to get up and shower. After a long, hot shower that did a lot to ease my headache, I went back to my room and got ready. I decided on my jeans and a black tank top with my black and silver flip-flops. Throwing my hair in a ponytail and my silver hoops in my ears, I decided I looked good enough for the ride home. I packed up my stuff so I would be ready when Ben was because he was not known for his patience even though he was known for his lateness.

I heard voices as I approached the kitchen and dining room area.

Rounding the corner, I saw the whole family, including the newlyweds, sitting at the large dining room table.

"There she is." Anna smiled. "We were just talking about you."

I managed a small wave and smile even though I was feeling a little self-conscious that I'd been the topic of conversation. "Morning, everyone."

"I was telling them how we met." Ben smirked.

I sat down in the only empty chair, which was between Grace and Jack, who immediately started putting food on my plate and barking at the boys to pass more.

"Yeah, so I was bombing this English Lit class because, come on, its stuff written by a bunch of dead guys, when the professor asked me if I wanted a tutor. I agreed, hoping she'd be hot." He paused, nudging Jake who was sitting beside him. "Guess we both got lucky, huh, Luce?"

Huh? I swallowed the yummy piece of omelet I'd been chewing. "Oh, yeah. Lucky, right." I looked toward Anna. "What is in this omelet? It is honestly the best thing I've ever tasted."

"Luce!" Ben yelled. "We're talking about our love and my hotness here."

I looked away from Anna, slightly annoyed. "Still?"

The laughter in the room was almost deafening. A lot of digs were yelled at Ben, including, "Yeah man, you definitely met your match," and others along the same lines. I looked at Ben, who was shaking his head, but I could tell he thought my disinterest was pretty funny.

"So, Lucy, Ben said you graduated this semester. What's your degree in?" Kasey asked.

"I have my Master's in Social Work," I replied around another bite.

"Wait. Your master's? How old are you, if you don't mind me asking?"

"I don't mind. I'm twenty-three."

"And you have your master's already?"

"She has a minor in English too," Ben bragged.

I looked around now while I sipped my coffee and realized everyone was waiting for me to talk. I always hated this part. Admitting my nerd status to a room full of who I was sure was always the popular crowd was more humiliating than normal.

"Yeah, I did classes through the summers and took extra credits throughout the semesters to finish early."

That was met with more stares. I didn't want to expound any more than that by admitting my social life was nonexistent until I met Ben. He brought that aspect of college to my boring life, but I still couldn't break the habits I had already created and therefore stayed on goal.

"Why did you want to finish early?" Grace asked.

"No real reason. Just ready to move on," I answered with a shrug.

Honestly, and what I didn't want to admit was that I'd never felt comfortable in school settings. I'd always been socially awkward in school, and college didn't lessen that, unfortunately.

"And tutoring this idiot didn't slow you down?" Jake smacked Ben in the back of the head.

Lucky for me, that ended the questions and started something of a wrestling match between the two brothers. They were then told by Jack to take it outside, which they did, along with most of the boys.

"Lucy, would you hold Mia for a second?" Kasey asked.

I held out my arms toward Kasey, who was holding Mia. "Sure, no problem."

I pushed my chair a little away from the table and stood Mia on my legs. She bounced up and down while playing with my earrings and laughing. I couldn't help laughing right along with her. Something about a baby's laughter had always been contagious to me. While trying to untangle her fingers from the end of my ponytail, I had the odd sense we were no longer alone. I looked around the room until my eyes settled on Christian, who was leaning in the doorway with his arms crossed over his chest, completely silent. His eyes and expression were completely blank. I swallowed hard past the lump in my throat as he approached me.

He stopped right by my chair and smiled down at Mia before directing his attention to me. "You guys getting ready to leave?"

A shiver traveled up my spine when I heard his voice, and it was clear I needed to leave. "Yeah, I think so." I paused, smiling down at Mia, who seemed determined to rip out my earrings. "What about you? Ben said you live in the area."

"Yeah, I'm heading out too. We all stayed this weekend to be on hand to help, but it's time to get back to real life now, you know?" His words held a lot more meaning than I think he even realized.

"Yeah," I whispered, lifting Mia to sit on the table with her feet resting on my legs.

"You never answered my question, you know."

I looked back up at Christian curiously. "What question?"

"What kind of relationship you have with my brother." He crossed his arms over his chest, making his biceps flex.

I let my eyes wander over them and imagined being wrapped up in those arms before traveling back to his eyes. I rolled my lips together and then bit down on the bottom one. He watched me the whole time with heated eyes, his arms unfolding until they were hanging at his sides, his hands rolled into fists and his jaw clenched. "What are you doing with Ben?"

"What?" I whispered, moving my eyes back and forth to look at his.

He leaned down closer to my face. "What—" Ben came barreling into the room, interrupting him. Christian backed up quickly and shot Ben a smile. "Have a safe trip back." He shoved Ben playfully in the shoulder when he passed. Ben turned to watch him leave, shaking his head and frowning before looking at me.

"You ready to head back?"

Absolutely.

The ride home was uneventful. Although, that came after an emotional goodbye with his family. There were a lot of hugs and "nice to meet you." Oh, and I can't forget the, "can't wait to see you next time." But the worst was, "maybe we can come visit you and Ben this summer."

"You know you need to tell your family we broke up, like soon, right?" I broke the silence that had been surrounding us thus far.

"Yeah, I will." That made me breathe a little easier. "Hey, sorry Chris was acting strange with you this weekend. I don't know what was up with him, except maybe the news, or no news I guess, about Cam." He reached over and tapped my thigh, saying, "Don't worry. I'm gonna say something to him about it."

"I don't think that's necessary, Ben," I answered quickly, not wanting to explain the few confusing moments Christian and I had spent together.

Even though Ben and I were only friends, I still somehow felt like I had done something wrong. I would never want to hurt Ben or Christian, and I had a feeling that our actions could do just that.

"I think maybe you should give him a break. This Cam stuff is probably affecting him more than you guys realize. I can't even imagine how I would be if I couldn't talk to Landon whenever I wanted."

Ben was quiet for a minute. "Yeah, you're probably right. I guess we'll let it go for now."

For now? Forever, I hoped.

Chapter Seven

Lucy

"Are you kidding me right now, Ben?" I shouted, unable to believe what he'd just told me. "What happened to telling them we broke up?"

Looking at Ben's guilty face, I realized what I should've realized a while ago. All those times I asked him how his family took the news of our breakup, he would shrug and say it went fine. I can't believe he did this. How dare he ask me to go home with him again? I was confused when he showed up at my place without even a text. He fessed up immediately, saying that his mom called him and had planned a Fourth of July party and wanted us to come home. I initially thought he meant as friends until his guilty face gave him away.

"One last time," he promised.

One last time, my ass. I was absolutely not doing that again. Walking right up to him, I poked him in the chest saying, "I am not doing that to your family again. No, Ben. My answer is no."

Shaking my head, I watched his face for a reaction, but I couldn't read his expression. "What? What's that face mean?"

"I already told them you were coming," he replied, hesitantly.

Bunching my hands into fists, I stared at my friend while anger rolled through my body. I'd never hit another person in my life, but I honestly thought I could at that moment.

I watched Ben's eyes widen when he looked at my fists, and he backed up a little, holding his hands up, palms out. "Whoa, hey there, killer. You gonna hit me?"

"I'm seriously considering it. Can you believe it, Ben? Look at me!" I yelled. "This is what you've turned me into. You've been lying to your family for over a month since the wedding. What exactly have you been telling them? What's next? Are we engaged too?" I couldn't stop yelling at him. "Ooh, I know. Maybe next I could be pregnant. How hard can that be to lie about, right?"

"Lucy, stop!" he yelled, surprising me. Running his hands through his hair, he turned away from me. "I'm sorry, okay. I'm sorry. I planned to tell them." I thought he might continue, but he stopped instead and turned to face me. "One last time, Luce. I swear. I won't ask you to do this again."

In my heart, I knew I couldn't do this again, not with the very real chance Christian would also be there. Oh, who was I kidding? Of course, he would be there, and I doubted very much that I could be cool, considering I hadn't stopped thinking about him since the last time I saw him. I couldn't tell Ben any of that to make him understand, though, and he seemed so desperate for me to go, but why?

"Are you going to explain to me why this is so important to you?"

With his hands on his hips, he looked at the ground. "I can't right now, but I need you to trust me. Please."

When he glanced up, he looked sad, and I felt myself caving. I didn't understand, but he was my friend, and for some reason, he needed this.

"One more time, Ben. But I swear if you don't tell them this time after we get back, I will. I can't keep lying to your family."

He nodded, but I hoped he realized how serious I was. I didn't feel right about this anymore.

Actually, I hadn't felt right about this since I'd danced with his brother.

Chapter Eight

Lucy

The fourth of July was on a Thursday, which worked out great because I had to work Friday night. We decided to go after work on Wednesday, and I would only stay for the party before heading back Friday morning. Unfortunately, I was still working two jobs—one as a waitress and the other as a bartender—while I waited for a response to the many applications I'd submitted. I'd thought by now, I would be settling in to my brand-new job, but no such luck.

We drove in separately Wednesday night because Ben had decided to stay the weekend. Our arrival was uneventful, minus of course the very excited welcome we received. I was relieved to find out that besides Ben and me, the only other person staying in the house was Grace and only because she was home from college for the summer, unlike Ben, who had stayed on campus to keep his job and take a summer class. He had decided to continue after graduation and get his master's in business. His end goal being to run the construction company that his dad and his uncles had started years ago. Jack had strongly encouraged him to get his business degree since the business had become much larger and involved commercial contracts as well as residential, according to Ben. As for his other brothers, they all lived locally and would be there for the day.

I didn't realize until the next day that what I thought was a family party was actually extended to many of their friends as well, making it a rather large event. I'd been introduced to family friends at the wedding, but because of how busy it was, I'd never really talked to them. I had the chance to see Jax, Kasey, and a few of the brothers, but avoided questions about Ben and our relationship as much as possible. Unfortunately, I realized that in order to do that, I had to keep to myself. Ben was also avoiding me a lot, but I assumed both of us were feeling guilty.

At one point, I found myself in the kitchen refilling trays and putting out drinks, looking for anything I could do to seem too busy to talk. I went in to fill the cooler with more juice boxes for the kids when I heard footsteps behind me. Crap. Please be anyone but Christian. I hadn't seen him yet on this trip, but I wasn't holding out much hope that it would stay that way.

"Hey, Lucy." I turned to see Jake sitting on a stool at the counter. I let out a relieved breath. That was okay. Jake I could handle.

"Hey, Jake. How's it going?" I turned back to finish putting the last few drinks in the cooler.

When he didn't answer I turned back around and noticed he had his head down with his forehead resting on top of his folded arms.

I immediately walked to him and put my hand on his shoulder. "Hey, are you okay?"

He lifted his head and rubbed the back of his neck. "No actually I'm not okay." Just when I thought that was all he would say, he surprised me by looking me straight in the eye, "Julie's pregnant."

I tried to school my reaction, but I've always had a terrible poker face, so it didn't surprise me when he huffed out a laugh, but it did surprise me that he was sharing something so personal.

"Yeah, that's pretty much how I feel." He shook his head. "What the hell am I going to do? I'm not cut out to be a dad.

I'm twenty-five and working construction for my dad. I haven't thought beyond who I'm drinking with tonight, let alone who I'm gonna be with tomorrow or hell, the rest of my life. Fuck, Lucy, I love my life the way it is. A kid's gonna change all of it." He sighed. "Sorry, I didn't mean to lay this all on you, but you're a good listener and you asked."

I reached out, took his hand, and leaned in toward him. "I get how this seems overwhelming right now, but as an outside person, I can promise you that you are not alone. I've never met a family like yours. The way you love and care for each other amazes me." I paused before continuing. "I can only imagine how much help and support you'll have. And, yeah, your life is going to change. But I'll bet all the good that comes with this change makes it worth it."

I attempted to pull my hand back, as he was just watching me. I felt like maybe I'd said too much, but he didn't let go.

"I see why you chose social work." I tilted my head at his words when he continued, "You're really good at making people see there's a light at the end of the tunnel."

I nodded, trying to hide my smile at the old clichéd saying, which seemed so odd coming from his lips. I was willing to bet he'd never said those words before in his life.

He smirked, obviously only hearing what he'd said after he'd said it. Before I could even respond, he added, "A pot of gold at the end of the rainbow."

Both of us were smiling wide now, and he snapped his fingers. "Every cloud has a silver lining."

There was no containing our laughter now, and we laughed for a while, both of us seeming to need the release.

I stopped laughing first but couldn't contain my smile when I leaned my hip against the side of the bar. "Are you done?"

He ran his hand along his jaw. "Yeah, I can't think of any more right now."

I nodded. "Those three were pretty good."

His smile grew. "In all seriousness, you are a great listener.

And you're one of those people who seems to know what to say to give hope when there isn't any."

"There's always hope as long as you believe in yourself. You just have to want something bad enough and then work really hard to make it happen," I replied.

"I never saw myself as someone's father," he admitted wearily.

"If it's worth anything, I think you're going to be a great dad."

His eyebrows rose. "Yeah? How do you know that?"

"Because you were raised by one. You don't know any different." I smiled at him, and his eyes softened when he smiled back.

He knocked his knuckles on the counter as he stood. "Thanks, Luce."

I smiled before he turned to leave and watched him walk outside. Poor Jake. A baby with Julie. The thought of a lifetime with Julie sent a shiver through me, so I couldn't even imagine what it was doing to Jake.

I made my way back outside for the beginning of the fireworks. I was feeling good that I'd been able to avoid a lot of questions about Ben, and if I went to bed right after the fireworks, I should be in the clear. I looked around for Ben but didn't see him, so I sat down with Grace on the grass. We chatted some about school and her semester coming up this fall. She was still undecided in her major but said she was considering some options. I didn't think she was ready to share those considerations yet with her family, though.

We watched the fireworks, oohed and aahed at the appropriate times, and enjoyed watching the kids get so excited. After the last of the fireworks had gone off, I decided to head inside. Jumping up, I gave Grace a hug goodbye because she said she was heading out to meet up with some friends, and I started toward the house.

I barely got through the front door when I heard loud voices. I'd learned with this family that loud voices didn't necessarily mean arguing. They did pretty much everything big and loud. Trying to avoid the living room where the voices were coming from, I quietly walked toward the stairs until I heard my name. They were talking about me?

I turned back around toward the living room when I heard more clearly, "What the fuck is wrong with you?"

Stepping through the doorway, I quickly surveyed the scene in front of me. What I saw was Christian facing off with Ben while Jack and Anna stood off to the side. I hadn't known Christian was here, considering this was the first time I'd seen him all day. The air in the room felt electric like there could be an explosion at any time.

"Ben?" I said.

All eyes shifted to me and sadness flickered through Ben's.

"Is everything okay?" I asked, hesitantly.

The silence was deafening as everyone looked between me and Ben.

"It's over, Luce." he answered quietly. "I'm sorry."

I heard Anna's gasp, but I couldn't look away from Ben. What the hell happened?

"That's it? That's all you're going to say to her?" Christian demanded.

"Ben, tell me what's going on. What's over?"

He sighed and looked down at the ground, shaking his head.

"Jesus, Ben, just tell her!" Christian yelled.

Ben's head snapped up, and he got in Christian's face who didn't back away. "Why don't you shut the fuck up? This is between Lucy and me. Nothing to do with you, man."

"That's where you're wrong, little brother. I'm the one who caught you, and if you don't tell her, I sure as hell will." Christian threatened.

"Why the fuck do you even care? You've been nothing but a prick to her since you met her!"

Christian grabbed the front of Ben's shirt in one hand and fisted his other one by his side. I looked at Jack and Anna, who continued to watch the scene playing out in front of them. Oh no, I didn't think so. I ran over to Ben and Christian and pushed my way between them, putting a hand on both of their chests. There was no way I'd allow something involving me to cause these two to fight. They didn't move, but they at least acknowledged me.

"Stop it!" I yelled. "This is ridiculous. You're brothers. What could possibly have happened to make you act like this?"

"He's cheating on you!" Christian snapped, never looking away from Ben.

Ben clenched his jaw and fisted his hands before he looked down at me with a guilty look on his face.

"I caught him when I got here and came in through the back." Christian continued this time, softening his voice and looking down at me. He looked back up at Ben, and sneered, "And with none other than Jackie! Isn't she fuckin' engaged?"

He gently pulled my hand from his chest and dropped it by my side before looking at Ben and shaking his head. He pushed Ben back and walked away. I looked at Ben and immediately felt bad for him. What a mess we'd made, and now he looked like a cheater in front of his family, which was one thing he would never do.

I turned around directly in front of Ben now, put my hands on his cheeks, and forced him to look at me. "It's time to tell them the truth," I encouraged softly. "You can't let them think this of you."

"What truth?" Anna looked back and forth between us. "What does that mean?"

Still staring at me, he nodded, and I gave him a small smile. I then grabbed his hand to show my support and to have his and stood beside him.

"Lucy and I aren't dating." He exhaled loudly.

"You broke up?" Anna asked.

Ben looked at his mom and shook his head.

"I don't understand," she admitted.

Ben dropped his head, and with his free hand, he ran his hand through his hair.

"We were never dating," I announced.

I looked toward Christian who had begun walking toward his parents and watched his body stiffen before he turned around. I quickly looked back at Anna, not wanting to see his expression.

"Why would you lie about that, Lucy? I don't understand." Anna repeated.

I closed my eyes and took a deep breath. "We—"

"Lucy did it as a favor for me." Ben interrupted before I could say more. "I asked her to come as my girlfriend to the wedding. I should've told you right after. She wanted to tell you the truth that weekend, but I wouldn't let her. None of this is her fault."

"That's not true, Ben. I went along with it. We share the blame," I admitted.

"But why?" Anna persisted.

"Ma, honestly, I had my reasons. And those same reasons applied to this weekend, but I'm not explaining them"—he looked directly at Christian—"to anyone."

Jack, who had been silent up to this point, looked at Ben. "Your reasons are your own, Ben, and we respect that. But next time, I suggest that you not involve a good friend and your family. Might be time to face the reasons head-on."

A silent message seemed to pass between Ben and Jack before Jack took Anna's hand and left the room. I glanced at Ben, but his eyes were locked on Christian, who watched us closely with his arms crossed over his chest, leaning up against the wall by the door. I decided it was time for me to leave and not only the room. I gave Ben's hand a squeeze and walked with my head down to avoid eye contact with Christian because yes, I was a wimp.

It was definitely time for me to go.

I tucked the little bit I had unpacked back into my bag, grabbed my purse and keys, and headed back downstairs. By this time, Ben was alone and staring out the window. I set my stuff down and put my hand on his back. He looked back at me and then turned and wrapped me in a hug.

"I'm gonna go," I said quietly.

"You don't have to."

"I think it's for the best. Give you some time alone with your family."

He nodded as I pulled back, but before I moved away, I looked up. "I'm not sure what your real reasons are, Ben, but I have a feeling they have something to do with whoever Jackie is. I just want you to know I'm here if you need me."

I started to back up when he grabbed my hand. "God, Luce, I'm so sorry about all of this. I never meant for it to go on this long." He paused, but his expression was pained. "Some things are hard to move past, you know?"

I nodded. "Yeah, trust me, I know."

"Yeah, I know you do," he admitted.

He looked past me and seemed to be lost in thought, but then said softly, "I need us to be okay. I can't lose you as a friend." He turned his eyes to me again, and I hesitated, not knowing what to do because he looked so destroyed. "Be careful. Text me when you get back, okay?"

I smiled a relieved smile, lifted to my tiptoes, threw my arms around his shoulders, and kissed his cheek. "That, right there, how you care about me, always making sure I'm safe, is why we will always be friends."

He smiled and gave me one more hug before I turned and left the room. I stopped in the kitchen, relieved to see no one was in there, and found a piece of paper and a pen. I was feeling fairly insecure, so a note sounded good to me. The truth was, I was too afraid to face them.

Jack and Anna,

I decided it would probably be best if I headed home tonight, but I wanted a chance to tell you again how sorry I am for all that happened. I promise our intention was never to hurt anyone even though it seems that's exactly what we did. Please know that I enjoyed every minute of my time with you and your family, and I appreciate all of your kindness. Ben is my best friend, and I would do anything to help him through what I thought was a tough time for him, but it should never have been at the expense of your trust. He loves and respects all of you so much, but I'm sure you already know that. I truly hope you can accept my apology for everything it is.

Love,

Lucy

I laid the note next to the coffee pot and took one more look around before grabbing my bags and leaving the house. Without a backward glance, I was in my car and had started the long drive home.

Alone.

Chapter Nine

Lucy

I woke to the sound of my doorbell and glanced at the clock. Three in the morning. Who the hell was ringing my doorbell at three a.m.? Ben. I jumped out of bed and ran to my door, never even checking the peephole, assuming something else must have happened with his family.

Throwing open the door, I stumbled back when I saw not Ben in my doorway, but Christian standing with his arms above his head resting on the doorjamb and an angry look on his face. He dropped his arms and walked toward me, effectively backing me into the room. The sound of my door slamming and the lock clicking in place made me jump back. He kept moving forward until my back hit the counter on the bar in my kitchen. He leaned forward and put his palms flat on the counter on either side of my hips until his face was right in front of me. I swallowed hard past the lump in my throat and tried to slow my breathing.

"You were never dating Ben?" His voice was low and rough. I opened my mouth to answer but immediately closed it. I didn't know how to answer. I'd had so many opportunities to tell him the truth but had always stayed loyal to Ben. I had no idea know how to explain that, how to make him understand, so instead, I shook my head and looked down.

"Look at me," he demanded.

When his fingers slid under my chin, I allowed him to lift it until our eyes met. "Did you fuck him?"

"What? No!"

He glared at me before he backed away and rested his hands on top of his head, his back turned to me.

When I finally found my confidence, I walked toward him. "Christian, what are you doing here?"

He spun around so quickly that I stumbled back again. "What am I doing here? You know what? I have no fucking clue!" Grabbing my arms, he pulled me until I was right up against him, chest to chest. "Do you have any idea what hell I put myself through wanting my brother's girl?"

He pushed me back with his body until my back hit the wall this time, his hands on landing on either side of my face. He pressed his body tight against mine, and I moaned. Have I ever wanted someone this badly before? I knew in my heart the answer was a resounding no. It hasn't made sense since I met this man, but every time I saw him or touched him, I craved him.

"Do you know what that feels like? All the fucking guilt? Knowing that you were with my brother and hating him for it? Hating him for meeting you first?"

He paused, dropping his head, and when he looked back at me, I saw guilt in his eyes before they moved to stare at my lips.

"Do you know that all I've been able to think about is what you taste like and how you would you feel under me?" He licked his lips and lowered his head until I could feel his warm breath fan across my lips. "Now I plan to find out."

He crushed his lips to mine, and I opened my mouth immediately to allow his tongue in to rub along mine. His hands came off the wall and circled my waist. Growling against my lips, he tilted his head and deepened the kiss. He pushed me closer to the wall, slamming his body against mine. Running his hands up until he was holding my head between his hands, tilting my head the way he wanted it. Moaning, I pushed back, needing to get closer. I needed to feel more. He ran his hands back down until he was cupping my ass and lifted me as I jumped enough to wrap my legs around his waist. Pulling our mouths apart, we were both breathing heavily when he pushed up and put pressure right where I needed it. I moaned and threw my head back against the wall while grinding against his cock.

"Room?" He growled.

I wrapped my arms around him when he started walking toward the hallway. "Left."

It wasn't long before I was thrown onto the bed seconds before his weight hit me. Oh my god, that felt good. He was hard, everywhere.

I ran my hands up and down his back and finally down to cup his ass in my hands. That seemed to spur him on even more because he grabbed the hem of my tank and pulled it up over my head. He groaned, and his tongue licked across my nipple while his hand palmed my other breast, pinching and rolling my nipple. When he wrapped his lips around my nipple and sucked, my back arched off the bed, and I hissed. My hands were in his hair, pulling at the soft strands. It seemed the harder I pulled, the harder he sucked.

I tried pulling his shirt off, but he brushed away my hands, then reached behind his neck and yanked it off, throwing it to the side. I ran my hands up his naked back and felt the muscles move and flex under them. His lips found mine again in a rough kiss while he pulled on my pants to push them down over my hips.

He paused and looked down, then hissed sharply and groaned, "No panties?"

He slid them down my body while pulling my pants the rest of the way off and throwing them on the floor. He jumped off the end of the bed, grabbed a condom out of his pocket, and threw it on the bed beside my hip. When he pushed his jeans and boxer briefs off and stood back up, my mouth went dry. Seriously, who was built like this? Scanning his body from his massive shoulders and arms down to his six-pack and then finally his long, hard cock, I couldn't quite catch my breath.

He looked down at me, saying, *"Sei più bella che mai immaginato,"* while he crawled back up the length of my body. If possible, that only made him sexier. I grabbed his head on either side and pulled his mouth back down to mine, wanting to taste those beautiful words on his tongue. His hard body felt so good against mine.

His hand traveled back down over my breasts before skimming along my stomach. My stomach clenched when his fingers floated over my clit and slid between my folds. He continued to kiss me while he slid his finger in up to his knuckle. I groaned and arched my hips, urging him to do more. He added a second finger when I ran one of my hands down his chest and held his cock in my fisted hand, stroking slowly.

"Fuck, baby, I can't wait. I need to feel you wrapped around my cock now." He emphasized this by rocking his fingers in and out, harder and harder.

"Yes, like that," I hissed.

He pulled his fingers out and grabbed the condom, ripping it open with his teeth. I squeezed his cock while watching him, which had him throwing his head back and groaning loud. I grabbed the condom from his hand and rolled it on myself, listening to the sounds of his heavy breathing. Running his hands down the outside of my thighs, he pulled my legs apart and pushed my knees up. He quickly lined his cock up and thrust in on a loud groan. Wrapping my legs around his hips, he grabbed my hips and slowly rocked his cock in and out.

"God, you're big." I groaned.

Truthfully, I was glad he was going slow because I could feel him stretching me to accommodate him. I had never been with anyone his size, but I was fairly certain he'd already ruined me for anything less.

"You can handle it. Fuck, you feel so good wrapped around me.

You're so fucking tight." He groaned out and smirked when his eyes focused on me. "You like when I talk to you like that, don't you?" I looked away, embarrassed by how much his words were turning me on. "Look at me."

Looking up at him, I saw the hungry look on his face when he thrust deeply and stopped moving. Leaning down until his lips were less than a breath away from mine, he whispered, "I need your eyes on me. I love feeling your pussy tighten around me when I talk to you."

He ground into me harder and rolled his hips when I gasped. He leaned in, kissing me again while he slowly started thrusting harder. Letting go of my hip, he ran one hand between our bodies and circled my throbbing clit, making me squirm and groan.

"Come for me," he demanded and rubbed his finger faster while his thrusting sped up.

"Harder. Please. Harder." I panted.

On a groan, he grabbed both of my hips, pulled them up, and changed the angle until he hit the perfect spot, thrusting fast.

"Christian, yes. Yes." I chanted.

He faltered but quickly got his pace again until the orgasm overwhelmed me, making me cry out. His thrusts become erratic while I was still tingling, and then he groaned loudly when he buried his face against my shoulder and pulled me tight against him. We lay still, waiting for our breathing to slow. I stroked his hair while he rubbed his hand up and down my side slowly, causing goose bumps to line my side and hip.

"Why do you call me Christian?" he asked so softly that I would have thought I'd imagined it if I hadn't felt his lips move against my shoulder.

Why do I call him Christian instead of Chris? The truth was, I had no idea. I simply liked the way it felt on my tongue. Not to mention, it had always felt more personal because no one else calls him by his full name.

"I don't know. I guess it feels more personal. Special somehow," I whispered. There I said it, and it felt good. No more lies. But the longer he remained quiet, the more embarrassed I became by my answer, so I followed up with, "Sounds stupid, right?"

He shifted until his face was in front of mine, staring at me with a look I couldn't decipher. My face got hot with humiliation, and he dropped his head so his forehead touched my chin. It didn't take long after that for the reality of what we did and where we were to set in. I knew he was leaving before he even pulled out. When he moved off me and left the room, a cold sensation overwhelmed me. I pulled my covers up over my chilled skin and sat up, leaning against the headboard. I watched Christian silently walk back into the bedroom and stare at me from the foot of the bed.

"I can't stay," he said.

I nodded, wondering what he wanted after this but too afraid to ask. I watched quietly as he got dressed. I thought he might leave without saying more, but before he walked out the door, he turned to me and said in a strangely distant voice. "I thought maybe, you know, because you hadn't been with Ben, but I can't."

"What can't you do, Christian?" I asked when I finally found my voice.

"I can't have anything with you," he muttered. Then looking me straight in the eye, he shook his head. "It's not worth it."

I flinched, but he didn't see that because he'd already turned his back on me and walked out. He also missed the hot tears that I tried so hard to swallow back as they finally broke free. I heard my door click closed before I got up and padded out to put the lock in place.

I wasn't worth it.

Sadly, that wasn't the first time I'd been told that.

But it would be the last.

Chapter Ten

Lucy

There came a time in everyone's life when we must choose our path. My choices lately had not been the best, and I was afraid those choices may have ruined the best friendship I'd ever had. I guess I should've had more faith in Ben because he texted me the next day before I left for work.

Ben: Hey. U good?

Lucy: Yeah. You? How r things with your folks?

Ben: OKAY. Think they're more upset that they've lost you. Pop said he knew all along-Ha. Plus, Jake told us Julie's pregnant so that took the heat off us.

Lucy: I'm glad it's worked out.

Ben: Sorry about how it came out. I didn't mean for that to happen the way it did.

Lucy: Yeah, I know. You gonna tell me about Jackie?

Lucy: Ben?

Ben: Yeah. Not ready yet.

Lucy: K. I'm here when u r. Still can't believe u cheated on me—lol! Love you

Ben: Love u

And there it was. All was forgiven. I should've known Ben's

family would understand. Well, all except one, but I couldn't think about that one. That was a choice I couldn't change, but I could regret and would for a long time.

All through the weekend, Ben and I texted, and he sounded better every day. He'd talked to his dad, so I assumed that had made all the difference in helping him feel better.

Monday came with a surprise when the director of Charlotte County's Children and Family Services called to offer me an interview. Of course I accepted but was hesitant. As much as I wanted to work in my field, the department was in New Hope. I'd put in that application so long ago—on the first trip to Ben's family home—that I'd forgotten about it.

Unfortunately, it was also the only offer I'd received, and I desperately needed to gain some experience or nobody else would hire me. She asked if I could be there Wednesday, and I agreed, but I didn't tell Ben in case I didn't get it. I knew if I got it and moved there, he would ask his family to help me get settled, and they would. That was just how nice they were. But I felt awful because I'd wanted to avoid that.

By Wednesday, I was so nervous that I almost considered canceling. I finally called Ben, who helped calm me down after he yelled at me for not telling him. By the time I got to New Hope, I was a little more relaxed. The director was friendly, which put me at ease, so the interview flowed smoothly. It was a small office, only employing five social workers because the county was small, and I would be the fifth. She explained that they were replacing a woman who had been with them for over twenty years and was retiring. We talked about the job, school, and then various other things until we realized we had been talking for almost two hours.

She offered me the job on the spot, saying she always trusted her gut, and she felt I was the perfect fit for their small team. Pushing all my doubts to the side, I accepted the position. I liked her. I wanted this. Plus, I was kind of tired of getting in my own way where happiness was concerned. This felt right, and I thought the move would be really good for me as long as I avoided any awkward situations with Ben's family.

Lucy: Hey. I got the job!!

Ben: I knew you would! When do you start?

Lucy: Two weeks. Have to do clearances and stuff.

Ben: Shit! You think those arrests for prostitution are gonna be a problem?

Lucy: Ha-ha.

Ben: We need to find you an apartment.

Lucy: Yeah.

Lucy: Gotta go. Landon's calling me back.

Ben: See ya.

I talked to Landon about my new job. As always, he was very supportive. He also said he needed a change and maybe would head my way for a while. I would love that, which I told him excitedly, and he promised to let me know soon. Landon had been traveling the world since we graduated, disappointing our parents. Not because he was traveling but because they didn't think his choices reflected well on them. He began by racing motorcycles and then doing stunt work in movies for a couple of years. He'd been injured in the last one about six months ago when he broke his leg in a jump. Unfortunately, because of nerve damage, he no longer qualified to do stunt work. He was now considered a liability. Helping a friend training guys to race and jump motorcycles kept him busy, but it became too hard on him to only be an observer. I could understand he needed a change.

Besides Ben and Landon, there wasn't anyone else to share the news with. I sent a quick message to my parents but hadn't heard back yet and truly didn't expect much. They'd never supported my goal to be a social worker.

The few friends I had in college had all either moved away for work or hadn't continued with their master's and went home. I didn't keep in touch, and they didn't either. I thought of Christian and realized my mind was not forgetting him as quickly as I would have liked. I didn't know if it was him, the sex, or the situation.

For whatever reason, he'd become a memory I couldn't shake. I was not at all experienced in these situations. I'd always been the girl with my nose in a book and always living in my brother's shadow. He was popular and fun. I was smart and serious. I hadn't even had a date in high school. Not because I didn't want one, but because no one had ever asked. College was better, as I'd made a conscious effort to look up every once in a while. That earned me a few dates and some sexual experience but not much. But when I went to my first college party, in my senior year, I met someone I wish had never noticed me.

Maybe that was why Christian was stuck in my brain. He was so intense and obviously knew what he was doing, but I needed to forget about him. He'd made it perfectly clear that I was not worth the effort, and I refused to feel that insignificant ever again.

Chapter Eleven

Lucy

New job. Check.
New apartment. Check.
Broke. Check.
Completely alone in a new city. Nope.

Thanks to Ben, his parents and sister had not left me alone, and it was obvious they had no plans to do so, considering I got my first phone call from Anna not even twenty-four hours after I got the job. She started the conversation by telling me that although they did not agree with our deception, they understood, and they've put all that nonsense behind them. I shook my head over the fact they were calling it nonsense. Anna continued to tell me how happy they were that I would be so close, which was very sweet.

Between the three of them, they sent me information on every available apartment they could find. Of course, Luke, a detective with the county police department, had to approve the area first. Even Jax, who I barely knew, checked the security in the buildings before I was even allowed to consider any.

As meddling as it all sounds, I appreciated it. Obviously, they were being helpful because it was important to Ben, but from my point of view, I needed all the allies I could get in a new city. I was excited when a few apartments passed their inspections, and I found one I liked. I talked to the landlord over the phone, who was kind enough to fax me the lease. I couldn't afford to make the extra trip, figuring I would already make at least two to move my stuff. My parents had agreed to pay for school, but everything else was my responsibility, and as much as I scrimped and saved, it still only stretched so far.

Before I knew it, the two weeks had passed, and I was packing up my life. Moving day was easy, considering I didn't have much. However, I was a little surprised when I opened the door to find both Ben and Jake standing there.

My eyebrows drew together. "What are you doing here?"

"What are you talking about? We're here to help you move." Ben seemed a little irritated.

I looked at Jake, who was smirking. "Hi, Jake."

"Hey, Luce. You guys gonna fight about this, or are we gonna get you moved?"

"I don't really have much to move. This apartment was furnished, so I don't have furniture to move. Only boxes and stuff. I figure most of it will fit in my car, and then I'll drive back tomorrow and pick up what's left." I shrugged.

"You're not doing that," Ben huffed and gently pushed me aside as he walked in with Jake right behind him. "Jake agreed to help you get it all in one haul."

Whatever. There was no point arguing since Jake was already here, so I started showing them what to carry down and finished boxing up what was left. After I sent the last few boxes down, I stood in the doorway and looked around. I hadn't expected to be sentimental about leaving, but it snuck up on me. Ben came up and leaned against my side, putting his arm around my shoulders, while Jake stood quietly on the other side.

"I still can't believe Chang let you break your lease," Ben admitted.

"I overheard him on the phone. Sounds like he's moving his girlfriend in," I answered.

"Wonder how his wife feels about that." Ben shook his head. "What a douche."

"Yeah, no kidding. It'll be nice to have a different landlord. That's for sure."

Ben placed both hands on my shoulders and turned me to face him. "You good?"

I looked away for a minute and let all the memories of the past five years wash over me. The good and the bad. The happy and the sad. The place where I discovered who I wanted to be and what I wanted to believe in. Bittersweet. That was the only word to describe today. I looked back at Ben and smiled.

Taking a deep breath, I nodded. "Yeah. I'm good."

He nodded and took my hand. Jake shut and locked the door behind us as we left the first place I had called my own.

I followed Jake back to New Hope because he knew a shortcut. It didn't seem any shorter to me, but I didn't say that, and we finally made it to my new place. My new landlord met us there with the keys and security codes for my apartment, along with instructions on how to set them with my own password. I had never lived in a building with a security system, so I was glad for the instructions. After he left and Jake and I hauled my stuff up, I offered him a drink before I realized I didn't have any drinks, which made us laugh.

"What about furniture?" He looked around at my empty space.

"I have some stuff coming." I lied. The truth was, after I paid my security deposit and first and last month's rent, my savings was gone. But if I told him that, then he would tell Ben and the cavalry would arrive. And I *would* have stuff coming, I just didn't know when.

Before he could question me further, I continued, "How's Julie?"

His face dropped a little at that, and I immediately regretted asking. "Well, she's definitely pregnant." He paused and then narrowed his eyes. "Even bitchier than normal."

Looking at him, I couldn't help but feel bad for him. Not because of the baby but because it didn't seem like Julie was making this easy on any of them.

"Can I ask you something that's none of my business?" I asked and waited for his nod. "What made you and Julie date in the first place?"

He took a deep breath, "Honestly?" When I nodded, he continued. "We were always only about the sex. I'm not even sure we liked each other, but the sex was off the charts." He smiled. "Guess now we are finding out if we like each other."

"I'm sure something else draws you two together, right?"

He smiled and shook his head. "You don't know much about being with someone exclusively for sex, do you?" he teased.

"Guess not." But I thought of Christian and remembered the most intense night of my life.

"Anyway, it doesn't matter now. We're going to be parents. That's what matters."

"You're going to be great, with or without Julie." I had my doubts that Julie would stick around for the long haul, unless maybe motherhood changed her. I glanced around my new place and sighed. "Well, I guess I should start unpacking, huh?"

Nodding, he said, "Do you need my help?"

"Nah, I'm probably better doing it alone, but thanks for everything. This pretty much monopolized your Saturday as it is, and I can't thank you enough." I reached up, because like Ben he was tall, and gave him a hug before walking him to the door. Closing it behind him, I looked around and smiled. I had a good feeling about this.

Walking around my apartment alone for the first time, I realized it was definitely bigger than my last one. The setup was similar, though, with the living room being what you stepped into immediately from the front door, which then led into the kitchen, so it appeared to be one big room. A bar with stools separated the kitchen from the living room, so I at least had something to sit on while I ate.

Walking past the kitchen, I saw a hallway, which consisted of a bedroom on one side and a bathroom right across on the other. Both rooms were actually rather large, considering it was only an apartment, and for the first time, I allowed myself to envision painting and decorating when I could buy paint and furniture. The pictures I'd seen hadn't done this place justice. It was charming, and it was clean, which was a huge relief. My old apartment had not been when I first moved in, and it had been a big project to clean and eliminate the smell. I never did find out why it smelled so bad, but I stopped trying to figure it out a long time ago. I probably didn't want to know.

My new place smelled like disinfectant, which solidified my thinking it had been thoroughly cleaned, but I still checked everything to be sure. Looking around the bedroom, I envisioned my bed, that I still didn't have but soon would, and thought of ways to make this my own.

Walking back out to the kitchen, I smiled and allowed myself to finally feel excited. Everything had happened so fast that I'd only focused on what I needed to accomplish so the move would go smoothly, but now that I had a minute to relax, I let it all settle in. I didn't know why, but this apartment, this job, and this town... they all felt right.

I let myself wonder for a moment what Christian would think of my new place but quickly squashed those thoughts. He wasn't a part of my life anymore. In fact, he really never was, and I've wondered recently if we were only ever meant to be a series of intense moments in time. The truth was, that relationship ended way before it began, if it truly ever had begun.

Looking over at the pile of boxes sitting on the floor in the middle of my living room, I decided it was time to stop thinking about my past and to move forward. That was what Christian was—my past. And although it would be difficult keeping him there while sharing the same town, I vowed to concentrate on my future and whatever that would bring.

Chapter Twelve

Lucy

Ben: Go get 'em!

This text greeted me Monday morning while I was getting ready for my first day of work. It made me smile and shake my head to imagine what Ben was doing right now. Summer classes had ended, which meant he was probably getting his schedule ready for fall. I heard from Anna that Grace had also headed back to school this past weekend when she stopped by on Saturday to invite me to dinner at their house on Sunday. I tried to decline but couldn't, considering all of my unpacking was done. Anna assured me attendance at the dinner would be small, as some of the family had other plans, so it wouldn't be weird for me to be there without Ben.

Yesterday, when I arrived, I was still nervous even though I saw few extra cars. Anna had said not to bring anything, but I felt strange showing up with nothing, so I decided to buy her flowers. If my memory served me right, there would be plenty of food. I wasn't sure what to wear for a family dinner, seeing my family had never had one, so I settled on a sundress and sandals. Hopefully, comfortable and casual was good enough.

I rang the bell and heard someone yell from inside to answer the door, which made me giggle. Everybody was always yelling here.

I looked up when I heard the door open and drew in a deep breath. Christian. I had secretly worried about this but couldn't explain it to anyone. I had hoped this would be one dinner he missed. When I had talked to Ben this morning and told him my plans, he'd said his mom did lunch *every* Sunday and those who could come, did, but it wasn't always everyone. She hosted it every week, so she saw her kids when they could make it. Unfortunately, it looked like he made it today.

"What are you doing here?" he asked without emotion.

"Your mom invited me. I just moved to town to start my new job." I looked behind him through the open door, hoping someone would come to see who was here, but no such luck.

He narrowed his eyes. "Yeah, I heard."

He seemed irritated by that information, which was starting to make me angry. I understood he regretted that night, but this was ridiculous.

I glanced behind him one more time before leaning in closer and whispered, "Look, Christian, I know we both regret what we did and realize what a huge mistake it was, but for today, can we just forget about it? Trust me, I wouldn't be here if your mom hadn't insisted."

He glared at me, moving in toward me, but before he could answer, I heard, "Christian. Move out of the way so the girl can come in."

Ah, Jack to the rescue. I smiled and walked through the door when Christian moved to the side, still staring at me. After getting hugs from everyone who was there, and Anna making a big deal about her flowers, we finally sat down to eat. Kasey sat on one side of me and Brody on the other, with Christian sitting right across from me. Because I was lucky like that. I sighed, which must have been louder than I thought because I heard Kasey giggle beside me before she looked down at her lap.

"So, Lucy, are you excited to start your job tomorrow?" Jake asked while Julie, who was sitting next to him, glared at me.

"I'm actually really excited. I talked to the director on Friday, and she said they already have cases for me to start on. They've been pretty backed up, I guess."

"Who is the director there now?" Jack asked.

"Her name's Marie Hastings. She said she's only been running things for about five years. I think the director before her retired. Actually, I'm replacing a woman who recently retired, and there are two more who I bet will do the same soon."

"I remember Marie from high school," Anna commented. "I'm ashamed to say it's been a long time since I've seen her, though. I had no idea she was the director there now. The last I heard, she had moved away with her husband. Something to do with his job, I think." She frowned. "You know, even though this is a small town, it seems we still don't see each other often because everyone is so spread out."

The rest of dinner was spent discussing people no one had seen in a while, which made me chuckle. During all of that, I tried to avoid Christian's eyes. They always seemed to be directed my way, so when I'd finally had enough, I gave up and stared back.

That was a big mistake. What had started as an angry stare down quickly turned into a heated gaze. I watched his eyes heat and then slowly move down to my mouth. I could feel my heart racing. How could someone affect me like that and so quickly? When his eyes returned to mine, I tried to look away, but as with everything else involving Christian, it was impossible. He was angry too, that much was obvious by the set of his expression. If it weren't for his eyes, I would have thought he hated me.

At that moment, I let myself feel anger for the first time. I'd blamed myself for so much when it came to Christian because I had deceived him by staying loyal to Ben, but he wasn't without blame. He came to me. And then he left me and never looked back. Never once did he consider his actions, and his words shattered me. I hadn't done those things to him.

I wished I could stop thinking about that night and comparing it to my other experiences. What would it be like if we had sex again? Would it be as intense? Or was that because of the situation? All I knew was when I was around him, my heart beat faster and there were tiny flutters in my belly. I could still remember every moment of that night. I felt my face getting hot while lost in the memories of his touch and the feeling of him inside me, moving over me, dominating me.

Lost in these thoughts and in the middle of a stare off with Christian, neither of us noticed the table had quieted. Kasey elbowed me in my side, and I glanced her way, immediately noticing Jack at the end of the table smiling at me. Oh, shit. Did I miss something he asked me? I looked at Kasey, who continued to stare across the table at Jax while grinning. Looking back at Christian, I noticed he seemed to have a silent conversation with Jack. What the hell did I miss?

"Aren't you with Ben? What the hell's going on with you and Chris?"

I looked across the table toward Julie, who was smirking.

"She's not with Ben, Julie. They're just friends," Jake replied impatiently.

"So, you're moving in on a different brother because Ben only wants to be friends?" she responded snidely.

Embarrassment made my face red, I shook my head and was about to defend myself when Jake spoke up. "That's enough Julie. She's not with anyone."

"Then why the hell is she even here?"

"Because I invited her." That came from Anna in a tone I had not heard from her before. And that tone was pissed. "And the last time I checked, this was *my* house."

Nobody said anything after that, but it was obvious dinner was officially over. Julie got up and left the table abruptly with Jake shaking his head, looking miserable. I excused myself to the bathroom upstairs to get a few minutes alone and pull myself together. Standing in the bathroom, I stared at myself in the mirror.

You can do this, I thought to myself. *Just forget about him.*

"Why can't I?" I whispered to the mirror.

"He's already told you he doesn't want you." I lectured myself. And I didn't want him. I just needed to remember his words and how much he hurt me.

With a sigh, I realized I needed to go back downstairs and face the family again. I opened the door and looked up, only to be face-to-face with my dream and my nightmare all rolled in to one ridiculously hot package. He pushed off the wall he was leaning against, and with a hand to my belly, he pushed me back into the bathroom and shut the door.

"What are you doing, Christian?" I whispered.

"What am I doing?" he asked, equally quiet. "What the hell are you doing?"

Confused by the question, I shook my head. Noticing he was getting closer, I backed up until I was against the wall behind the door. Being that close to him was a bad idea.

"What the fuck are you doing to me?" he growled when he reached me. He put his hands on either side of my head and leaned in until all I could see was him. "Why can't I forget you?" He spoke but almost as if he was talking to himself.

Being that close, I forgot my resolve to stay away from him. I could feel his heat envelop my body like a blanket. He didn't want me. Or at least he didn't want to want me. This may be my chance to discover if my memory was accurate, or if I made him to be something more than what he was. My last chance to feel him, taste him, and I wasn't going to miss it. Moving toward him while rising to my toes, I watched his eyes darken and his lips part. Not needing more of an invitation, I leaned in and touched my lips to his. I felt him groan before I even heard it while his hands moved to rest on the sides of my face. Moving my lips slowly, trying to memorize his lips and taste, I put my hands on his chest. I wasn't sure when the kiss changed or who even initiated the change, but when it did, it became wild.

Uncontrollable.

Our lips both opened, and he thrust his tongue into my mouth while his hands moved from my face to my hips. He pulled me into him forcefully, rocking his hips, and I ground myself against him shamelessly. I needed more skin. Pulling his shirt up in the back, I slid my hands up his back and over smooth, hard muscle. He groaned again, louder this time, and used his hands to pull down the front of my dress but only enough to reveal my breasts and rub his thumbs over my hard nipples. I moaned at the feel of his hands and pushed my hips farther into his. He grabbed my thigh and pulled my leg up, my dress bunched around my waist, and I shivered at the increased contact.

He broke the kiss when it became impossible to breathe and ran his tongue down the side of my neck. I arched my back and neck, giving him room and also increasing the growing pressure between my legs. I needed him so badly that I ached. Knowing only one thing could help, I rubbed myself shamelessly up and down his thigh, pushing harder on each pass to increase the pressure on my clit. His fingers continued to pull at my nipples, pinching them and then soothing with small strokes.

"Christian." I moaned, which brought his mouth back to mine for another wild mating of our lips. His hands moved down my body, over my stomach, until one slid down and over my panties, covering my mound. I hissed and pulled him closer to me, breaking the kiss while panting.

"Lucy." I heard the knock on the door. "Honey, are you okay?" Anna spoke with concern.

Panting, I looked up at Christian who still hadn't moved his hand. I stared at him with wide eyes and then looked at the closed door. I pulled on his wrist to get his hand to stop moving, but he wouldn't budge. Embarrassed now that I had forgotten where I was, I pleaded with my eyes for him to stop, but he increased the pressure with his hand until my eyes closed and my back arched.

"You better answer her," he whispered. Then he went back to

rubbing his palm over me and brushing against my clit with each pass.

My eyes flew open, and I met his. What? I couldn't even catch my breath, let alone form a complete sentence.

"Lucy?" she called again.

"Umm yeah, Anna, I'm okay," I answered, staring daggers at Christian who was smirking as he continued to rub me.

"Are you sure, honey? You sound out of breath."

"Yeah, could you give me another minute?" I yelled.

"Of course," she said. "Let me know if you need anything."

I tried to listen for her to walk away, feeling guilty that I was essentially dry humping her son in her house, but I was so close to climaxing that I suddenly didn't care where I was or who heard.

"Christian." I panted and leaned my head back against the wall. "I need to come." I pushed on his wrist until the pressure from his palm was almost painful, but it still wasn't enough.

"Yeah, baby. I need that too. I want to watch you come, knowing all it takes is a kiss and my hand rubbing your pussy."

I whimpered when he increased the speed of his hand. Reaching forward, I grabbed a fist full of his shirt and pulled him to me, pressing my lips to his and shoving my tongue in his mouth. He took his finger and moved my panties to the side to flick his finger over my clit. And I exploded. He kept his mouth on mine, absorbing my scream. My body arched and trembled through one of the hardest, most intense orgasms of my life. I rested my head back against the wall, eyes closed, and tried to catch my breath. He continued to hold me, his hand caressing me over my panties now and I opened my eyes, but I couldn't look at him. I fixed the top of my dress to cover myself and felt him release my leg and pull his hand free. Looking up at him, I was immediately overwhelmed with shame. What was I doing? As if reading my thoughts, he backed up and turned away from me, running his hand through his hair. What did he expect now? Did he want me to return the favor?

Feeling confused and embarrassed, I cleared my throat. "Umm, I'm not sure—"

"Don't say anything." He cut me off. "What the hell is wrong with me?" I heard him whisper but knew he wasn't asking because he needed or wanted an answer.

"I'm gonna go," I said, hoping for a response, anything. He didn't answer. He didn't even turn to look at me. Standing in front of the door, I turned to leave but holding my hand on the knob, I spoke quietly, "You know, you said I'm not worth this, and you were right." I paused, building my nerve to continue. "I'm worth a hell of a lot more than this."

I wasn't sure if I was doing the right thing. I had never been in this situation before, but I knew I needed to get out of there, so I left. I shut the door behind me, hoping with a small part of me that he would open it and pull me into his arms. But I knew that would never happen. This had been a mistake. We obviously have strong chemistry between us, but every time we've acted on it, we've regretted it. The truth was, he would never see me as anything but Ben's Lucy.

I went back downstairs and walked into the dining room where everyone sat talking. The table became very quiet, and I simply stood there, having no idea what excuse to give for my absence. Then Kasey got up and started clearing away the dirty dishes. I jumped right in to help, happy to have something to do thanks to Kasey. When we finished, we stayed in the kitchen and cleaned up there. We heard parts of the conversation in the dining room, which consisted mainly of Jake apologizing to his parents and brothers because of Julie's behavior.

"Man, she's a bitch," Kasey muttered while I washed the dishes that wouldn't fit in the dishwasher, and she dried. "I can't believe she talked to you like that, and believe me, it really pissed her off when both Jake and Anna jumped to defend you."

"I feel sorry for Jake," I admitted.

"Yeah, me too. I'm not sure what he was thinking when he got with her."

He'd obviously told me what he'd been thinking, but I wasn't going to share that with Kasey. I wasn't sure she would keep it to herself, and I didn't want to betray Jake's trust.

"So, you and Ben? You were really never together?" she inquired.

I looked over at her while I rinsed a dish and shook my head. "Nope. Always just friends. Actually, he became like a brother to me. I can't imagine being anything but friends with him."

"And Chris?" she probed.

I looked out the window in front of me and felt my face heat. I would've loved to share with someone what happened with me and Christian, if for no other reason than to get it off my chest. I wished I had a girlfriend to share with, but I wasn't sure if that could be Kasey yet. She was too involved with the family. I'd already made enough bad choices concerning this family, so I wasn't going to make another one by putting Kasey in an awkward position with Jackson.

"I don't know Christian very well," I replied quietly.

"You guys were staring at each other pretty intensely. I mean, you didn't even notice when everyone else was quiet and watching you." She giggled.

I left out a loud breath, "Yeah, I know. I think he's still upset about the whole Ben thing."

She put her towel down on the counter and turned toward me. "For what it's worth, everyone else is over it. Initially, we were all happy to see Ben so happy, and you two do make a cute couple, but honestly, you acted more like friends than lovers."

She paused, and I waited, sensing she had more to say. "I know we don't know each other very well, but I'd like to change that. Especially since you're in town now. You know, go to lunch or the movies. Maybe a girls' night out," she said excitedly.

"I'd like that," I answered honestly.

After we finished up the remaining few dishes, we found our phones to exchange numbers before Kasey grabbed Jackson and Mia and headed home. I also said I was going to head out but not before Anna stopped me to say she was sending food with me. I told her she didn't need to, but she shook her head and kept bagging stuff. I hugged both Jack and Anna and told them how much I appreciated their thoughtfulness. They, of course, invited me next Sunday, and I told them I would call and let them know.

I already knew I was going to miss.

Jake pulled me aside and apologized for Julie's behavior, which I told him didn't bother me and not to worry about it. He didn't look convinced but hugged me and promised to check on me later. I looked up at Brody, who was standing near his dad, and he gave me a chin lift while he smirked. I gave him a small wave and smiled. I wasn't even sure if he spoke today. I got to my car and put all the leftovers on the back seat before standing back up and closing the door.

I felt him before I saw him. I turned around slowly only to realize he had me backed up against the driver's door. He put his hands on the car right beside my arms and leaned down until we were eye to eye. Breathing heavily, I was suddenly embarrassed, considering he didn't look bothered at all. At least not physically. But he did look angry. I could feel his warm breath on my lips, which made me close my eyes and roll my bottom lip between my teeth. When I opened my eyes, he was staring down at my lips, but he must have sensed I was watching him because he looked up at me.

"You weren't supposed to be here," he growled and looked down at my lips again. "Not here."

"Then let me go," I whispered.

His head jerked up, and his eyes met mine. I blinked hard to keep the tears away at least until I could get in my car. He backed up and dropped his arms to his sides while I quickly got into my car, started it, and backed out of the driveway. I didn't look back. I didn't see Christian watching me drive away, or his dad standing in the window shaking his head.

I shook my head to clear the memories. Today was the first day at my brand-new job, so I needed to stay focused.

Chapter Thirteen

Lucy

I couldn't believe I'd been here a month already. Thankfully, my new apartment had a washer and dryer, and I'd finished doing my laundry. I still didn't have much furniture. My bed was still an air mattress, which wasn't that bad, considering the alternative was the floor. I'd been saving up for living room and bedroom furniture but needed to get necessities first, which left me almost completely broke. Things were starting to look up now, though.

My first few cases at work had been challenging. Social work was definitely a steep learning curve, as every case had been very different and required a different approach. One concerned me, though, because the dad gave me the creeps. He would only stare at me while I was talking to him. And it wasn't in the "I'm interested in what you're telling me" way either. It was more the "make your skin crawl" way. I truly needed to look past it because he had a daughter, and I was more worried about her safety than mine. So far, I'd only had to monitor. He'd also proven to know the Child Protective Services rules well during our visits, but I doubted he understood the reach CPS had to ensure his daughter's safety. Mrs. Hastings told me he had been on their radar for a very long time, but a recent charge of possession of drugs caused an arrest that finally allowed us in to monitor the situation. He was currently on probation, which fortunately included CPS involvement.

I hadn't been back to Jack and Anna's for dinner. Each time, I would tell them I was swamped with my caseload, which wasn't exactly a lie, and trying to get settled. They'd been accepting of this, but I had a feeling my reprieve wouldn't last for much longer. I'd been talking to Ben but not as much because he had started classes. They were master's level, so they took up a lot more of his time. I'd also talked to Kasey a few times but told her I was unable to do anything for the same reasons. She seemed understanding so far.

I'd been fortunate to make friends at work. They were open and had helped me learn the area and people. I'd even agreed to go out a few times after work with two of my co-workers, Sam and Molly. Sam was the only man in our office, so I think he tried extra hard to get along. I was sure he didn't want to get on the bad side of four women. Just thinking about time spent with Sam and Molly made me smile. So far, this move had been exactly what I'd hoped for.

I'd only just started a grocery list when my doorbell rang, and I assumed it was the older lady next door who had started coming over on Saturdays. She seemed lonely with no family close by, and I could empathize. Answering the door, I recognized my stalling had ended because Kasey stood there with a very determined look on her face.

"Don't say anything. I'm taking you to lunch today and then either the movies or to get our nails done. I'll let you pick which," she stated sternly.

I couldn't help but laugh out loud, which seemed to soften up her features but only a little. She barreled past me into my apartment and quickly stopped. "Where's all your furniture?"

"There was a mix-up at the store. It's coming soon." Damn, I hated lying, but I didn't need or want any sympathy gestures. I was still standing behind her, which was good because at least I wasn't lying to her face. She turned to look at me, gauging my answer.

Whatever she saw must have satisfied her because she moved on.

"Okay, so which is it?" She arched an eyebrow and put a hand on her hip.

I thought about my budget and then looked down at my nails. Oh, what the hell. "Nails, definitely."

She clapped and danced around excitedly. "Well then, let's go. I left Mia with Jax, and I don't know how much time I have until he calls in a panic about something."

That sounded unbelievable to me, as he seemed so confident. When I said this to Kasey, she laughed. "Oh, he is. About everything, but Mia. He's always afraid he's doing something wrong." She shook her head. "The last time I left them alone so I could get my hair highlighted before the wedding, he called his mom when Mia refused to eat. Now remember, he has fed her before, but it's like once he's alone, he forgets everything. Anyway, he was trying to get her to eat green beans, which she hates and refuses every time." She laughed and shook her head. "He couldn't get ahold of me, so he called his mom who knows he does this every time I leave, and told her something was wrong because Mia wouldn't eat." Now she was full on laughing. "And you know how sweet and helpful Anna is, right?" I nodded. "Well, she told him to suck it up and figure it out because she raised eight kids with nobody to call. Then she hung up on him and high-fived me." She nodded when I widened my eyes. "Yep, she was with me getting her hair done, and nobody interrupts Anna getting her hair done. We laughed the rest of the time we were there."

"What happened when you got home?" I had to know.

"He was so mad at his mom. Went on and on about how he can never rely on his family for anything and he wasn't going to dinner on Sunday. Of course, we did, and he glared at his mom until his dad told him to knock it off and grow up."

"Now all is well?" I laughed along with her.

"Oh, Luce, it was fine the next minute because Jake came in with Julie, and everyone ganged up on him for a while."

"Wow, this family is genuinely crazy, aren't they?"

"They're amazing," she responded, wearing a small smile. "I couldn't have asked for anything better to marry into. I was an only child, but I never realized how lonely that was until I met Jax. Now I'm the one dragging him to all the family things to see what happens next."

"Just so you know, I don't think all families are like them. I mean, I grew up with a brother, and my house and relationships were never like theirs," I said.

"Aren't you close? Not even with your brother?" She frowned.

"I'm very close to my brother. He's also my twin." She raised her eyebrows at this. Apparently, she didn't know. "But my parents kind of keep to themselves. I've always wondered why they even had us, considering they seem to like their work more."

"That's so sad."

"It's okay, really. It's something we've always known, and at least, I have Landon," I answered happily.

She nodded, and we left to head to lunch. Kasey took me to a restaurant near the nail place where she's always gone. On the way, she told me how her family moved to New Hope when she was a senior in high school because her dad had a job transfer.

"I didn't want to move here and leave my friends, but we didn't have a choice. After I finished high school, I went to college about an hour from here to get my teaching degree and was lucky enough to be hired at our local elementary school almost right out of college."

"So you wanted to come back here after college?" I asked.

She nodded. "Yeah, I fell in love with this town and the people. We had moved here from the city, and I was surprised by how much I liked the small town. I didn't miss the city at all like I thought I would." She paused and laughed. "Well, maybe the shopping, but that's about it."

"So how did you meet Jax?" I was curious since she hadn't mentioned him yet.

LUCY

She smiled softly. "The school had the local heroes come talk to the kids about their jobs. I was voted to head this project somehow, along with a few co-workers, so we asked the local fire department and the police department if anyone would be interested in talking to the kids during an assembly. We had quite a few volunteers, which was wonderful. When a call came from the police department suggesting we have local soldiers not currently deployed also come and share, we were thrilled and a little ashamed we hadn't thought of that already." She grimaced. "Luke had been the one to make the call and basically volunteered Jax even though he hadn't agreed yet."

"So what happened? Was he mad?" I inquired curiously.

She sighed. "I don't think he was mad, but he had just left the Navy and was still settling in to life as a civilian, so I'm not sure he felt he was in the right headspace to talk to the kids. Anyway, he came and was short with me when I introduced myself and explained the plan for the assembly. I didn't like his attitude and told him as much. We had an argument and ended up making out in the janitor's closet before his turn to talk at the assembly."

I was picturing that and giggling when Kasey joined in. "Yeah, probably not a shining moment in my teaching career, but it led me to the best thing that ever happened to me, so I honestly can't regret it." She shrugged.

Pulling into the restaurant, I glanced her way. "What an amazing story. Will you ever tell Mia how you met?"

"Maybe that we met at school and why, but I will *never* tell her what I did in that closet," she answered, laughing the whole time.

Still chuckling while we walked into the restaurant, I realized I was having a really great time. I couldn't remember the last time I laughed this much.

After we were seated, we both ordered chicken salads without even looking at the menus, which Kasey said we're the best in town. Lunch was spent with her telling me about all of Ben's brothers, and I realized how much I didn't know.

"So you never told me where Jackson works? Wait, or should I call him Jax? This is like Christian or Chris?" I laughed.

She laughed. "It's actually any of the above. Some of the family says Jackson, some say Jax, and they mix it up sometimes too. Same with Christian. You can say whatever. As far as Jax's work goes, he and Brody own a company that creates and implements security systems. It was part of their specialty in the military, so they've found a way to transfer it into a career."

"Wow. I didn't know that. That's amazing."

"Yeah, and they're really good at it. They're actually in demand now because of their reputation. Once Chris came home last year, they recruited him as well because they needed more guys."

"So Christian was military too?" I was surprised I hadn't already known that.

"Yeah, Jax and Brody were in the Navy, and Chris was a Marine."

"What about Cam?" I asked.

Kasey's face fell a little before she responded with a sad smile. "Cam and Chris enlisted together. They were always together. As long as I've known them, where one went the other went. As far as I know, they served together for a while before they were split up due to their skills. Cam was…" She stopped and shook her head. "*Is* a tracker. One of the best, so he was moved to an elite team. Christian's sniper skills took him to a different team."

I was afraid to ask the obvious next question because maybe it was too personal, but luckily, I didn't have to.

"Chris was injured by an explosion on his last tour. He ended up with damage to his left eye, which essentially ended his career. It's better now, but he was discharged right after. Brody and Jax hired him right away and taught him their security systems, and he's been an amazing addition to the team. Jax said he still has reduced distance vision, but he's fine up close. It doesn't seem to affect his work."

I frowned. "Was he upset to be discharged?"

"It seemed he was more upset leaving and not knowing where Cam was. No one would tell him anything. Actually, no one has said anything to anyone, and we haven't heard from Cam for a while now."

I tried to imagine what that must be like for him, for all of them, seeing how close they all are. I looked at Kasey. "That's so sad. I can't even imagine."

Kasey nodded and then smiled. "I refuse to make our first day out sad! I'm sorry I even started all of that. Let's finish our lunch and get our nails done."

I smiled and nodded even though my heart was breaking for all the brothers but especially Christian.

Chapter Fourteen

Lucy

I zipped my jacket before leaving the office as I already knew from my earlier home visits it was chilly out. Winter had hit the East Coast a little sooner than usual, and the colder temperatures came quickly. After only a little more than three months in New Hope, I'd felt like I'd lived here a lifetime, and I loved it. I loved the town and the people, some with whom I was on a first-name basis. I even loved my job on most days.

Today hadn't been the best day. I'd had a home visit with Mr. Mills, the dad on probation, and again, he was behaving strangely. But I spent some time with his daughter, and she appeared fine. Surprisingly, the house was in better shape than I'd seen it before, and there was plenty of food. This was a small town with a lower caseload, so I was often able to spend more time with the kids on my list. Today, I spent time with Morgan and played a game. I was trying to get a better read on her and her dad, but she wasn't talking much. I made a mental note to spend more time with her, and I also considered seeing her at school.

I was out of the building and ready to close the door when I realized I forgot my purse. Turning to go back in, I saw a flash of a person disappearing around the corner of the building. That was strange.

I'd been having odd feelings of being followed lately, but they always seemed to coincide with the days I visited the Mills' family, so I'd chalked it up to being a little paranoid. I grabbed my purse and went to my car quickly. Driving home, I checked my rearview mirror a few extra times and then shook my head and laughed at myself. I think I was letting some strange situations with one case go to my head. Thank goodness it was Friday. I definitely needed a weekend off. My plan was to go furniture shopping, finally. Arriving home, I decided on a hot shower first to wash away the anxiety of the day and then dinner.

I'd just finished dinner and was searching for a new book on my Kindle when I heard my phone beep.

Ben: Miss me?

I laughed out loud.

Lucy: Nope

Ben: Liar

Lucy: ha ha. What's up?

Ben: just wondered what u r doing tonight.

Lucy: hot date

Ben: Hmm…really? Is that him at the door?

I looked up when my doorbell rang and then heard my phone beep. I looked down and smiled. Jumping up, I ran to the door and flung it open.

"Surprise! It's your hot date," Ben said as I launched myself at him for a hug. I hadn't realized how much I missed my friend until right now.

"What are you doing here?" I asked excitedly, moving back to let him in.

"Well, I figured without me around you were probably staying home and"—he frowned—"reading."

I laughed. "You say that like it's a dirty word."

I caught his frown as he turned a full circle in my living room. "Um, Luce, where's your furniture?"

Why was his family so concerned about my furniture situation?

At least this time I didn't have to lie. "Actually, I'm going shopping for it this weekend."

"Why haven't you had any before now?" he asked, seriously.

"Relax." I smiled at him. "I wanted to wait until I was financially able and knew I wasn't going to get fired."

"Okay, well I'm going along to haul it back for you. When are we going?"

"You really want to spend your Saturday shopping for furniture?"

He smirked. "Actually no, but I also know you've been telling everyone you have furniture coming, and it hasn't arrived yet."

Those snitches. "I'm planning to go this weekend."

"Good, then you won't mind some company."

"Please tell me that's not the only reason you're home." I couldn't believe he came home to lecture me on furniture, but Ben was unpredictable, and even though he could've done this over the phone, it wasn't that unreasonable to see him in my apartment.

"Nah. I had planned on it anyway. I think Ma's missing her favorite." He smiled and wiggled his eyebrows.

I rolled my eyes, and we both laughed.

"Come on. Go get dressed. I told my brothers we'd meet them at Mac's for a beer."

I'd found out last month from Kasey that Mac's was a neighborhood bar the boys had been going to since they were twenty-one and probably before. I agreed and changed from my PJ's to some jeans and a sweater with my brown knee-high boots. Knowing that Ben was not patient, I threw my hair in a ponytail and put on a little makeup.

"All ready!" I yelled as I walked back out. I got an approving head nod, at least that was what I assumed the head nod meant, and he dragged me out the door.

When we walked in, I realized my mistake of agreeing to this without asking questions. He'd said brothers, but I didn't think he'd meant all his brothers. I gave everyone a small wave when they shouted out to me as they were doing the back-slapping thing with Ben. When the waitress came to the table, the guys all ordered a beer, and Ben ordered me a vodka and orange juice, knowing I didn't really like beer.

"You don't drink beer, Luce?" Jake inquired.

"Not usually. I've never been much of a beer drinker." I met Christian's hard gaze down the table and sighed. Damn Ben. Why did he even bring me with him? I leaned over to Ben, who was sitting beside me, and whispered, "I think I'm going to go."

His eyebrows drew together. "Go where?"

"Home."

"We just got here. Why do you want to go already?"

"Hey, are you sure you two aren't dating? You look pretty cozy," Luke teased.

I looked up at him and smiled, noticing the hard glare from Christian sitting beside Luke. "I was just telling Ben that I think I'm going home." I gestured toward Ben. "He didn't tell me it was a boy's thing tonight."

"At least stay for one drink," Ben pleaded. "I didn't know it was only the guys tonight."

When the guys all agreed, I said I would stay for one drink. I listened to them tease each other, talking about nothing in particular. Jax, who was on the other side of me, told me a story about Kasey and Mia, which was very funny. I was amazed to see how much he loved them, and it was obvious not only in the way he told the story but also in the expression he wore.

We were laughing together when we noticed the table had been surrounded by women. I felt ridiculous right then in my jeans and sweater when I saw what they were wearing. Skirts the size of tube tops, and what could pass for bikini tops as shirts, and yep, stilettos. Not boots. Weren't they cold? They were completely ignoring that I was even sitting at the table, so I could only assume they felt I was no competition. I excused myself, only to Jax, because no one else was even looking at me, and went to the bathroom.

I looked in the mirror and sighed. I'd tried to be as outgoing as those girls when I first started college, but I couldn't do it. I'm not very good at flirting or wearing short, tight clothes, so I stuck with what I knew. I'd dated a little but always in my league and never going out of my comfort zone. Honestly, if these guys weren't Ben's brothers, I wouldn't even be sitting with them or talking to one of them, let alone all six. I think the only reason I could spend time with Ben initially was because I was tutoring him and that felt safe.

I pushed open the bathroom door and was surprised to see Christian standing against the wall with his arms crossed over his chest. Still glaring at me. Part of me wanted to just walk by him, but that would clearly be immature, and I wouldn't give him the satisfaction. The hallway where the bathrooms were located was dark and stuffy, which added to this already uncomfortable situation.

I stopped walking right in front of him and tried a small smile. When I got no response, I sighed and turned to walk away. He grabbed my arm and swung me around until my back hit the wall, and he was right in front of me, hands on the wall beside my head, boxing me in. When my breath hitched, I closed my eyes. I had to tell him to stop doing this to me. When I opened my eyes, his face was close to mine, and his breathing was also fast, so I assumed he was angry with me again. But then he moved his head until it was beside mine with his lips near my ear. His breath felt hot against my face. He smelled amazing, and it reminded me of being outside on a fall day. I shivered when he slowly ran his nose along the side of my cheek. I stood perfectly still, wanting him to keep going and thinking if I didn't say anything or move at all, he would stay here with me. His forehead rested against my shoulder, but I realized he still hadn't moved his hands to touch me in any other way.

At that moment, it was obvious he felt something for me but would never allow more because of Ben, or maybe because of me. I'd never been worth the fight for someone. Never been the one someone would change plans to spend time with. I'd never been enough. He'd even told me that, but my mind kept blocking it like it hadn't been said. But it was, and I refused to allow myself to hope any longer for something different with Christian. A few amazing moments was all we could be because he believed I'd had something with Ben, and I couldn't change that. But I could change how I'd responded. I couldn't spend the rest of my life wondering and waiting, hoping that maybe this time he'd think it was worth it.

With pride fueling me, I put my hands to his chest and softly pushed to back him up. His head jerked up, and he looked down at me with a frown on his face. No words needed to be said. He seemed to know that I had finally found the courage to draw a line between us. He backed up and dropped his hands to his sides. With one last look in my eyes, he turned and walked back down the hall toward the bar. I stood there for a while with my head leaning against the wall and my eyes closed. I could hear people coming and going, but I never even opened my eyes. I couldn't understand why I felt like I lost something I never really had.

I made my way back out to the bar as I realized if I spent much more time away, someone else may come looking for me. I didn't want to explain my meltdown in the hall to anyone, especially Ben. The minute I turned the corner from the hallway where the bathrooms were, I knew no one was looking for me. More girls had arrived, and my seat was officially taken. I looked around the table and shook my head at the guys and their antics until I got to Christian. A girl was leaning down and whispering something in his ear and at the same time giving him an eyeful of impressive cleavage. I couldn't distinguish the look on his face, but I figured they would be going home together. I put my head down and bit my lip until I realized what I was doing. I've been trying so hard to break that habit. I looked for Jax but didn't see him, so I assumed he left. We had brought my car because I agreed to be the driver, guessing Ben would be leaving with someone anyway. I grabbed my phone and sent him a quick text letting him know I left and would see him later before I dug my car keys out and walked quickly toward the exit.

It wasn't until I was outside that I remembered we'd had to park at the back of the parking lot because the lot was small, and the bar was crowded. I looked around because I had that strange sensation again that someone was watching me, but I didn't see anyone.

Almost halfway to the car, I heard a shuffling sound, like shoes on pavement, and turned my head to look behind me when I saw someone out of the corner of my eye. I started running, knowing this time I wasn't just being paranoid when I heard his footsteps getting closer. I ran faster. My breathing sounded loud in my ears, but no louder than my heartbeat. It felt like my heart was trying to beat right out of my chest. I was running between parked cars when I cut across and headed toward the exit where my car was parked.

I heard a car horn and looked left to see that I had run out in front of a car turning to head out of the lot. I waved an apology and ran the rest of the way to my car, which wasn't far, and quickly got in, locking the doors. Maybe I should've stopped that car I ran in front of, but I didn't recognize the driver. I was breathing hard and looking around but saw nothing again. I didn't understand because I'd definitely heard footsteps. Too afraid to get back out of my car and cross the parking lot again, I decided to hurry home, then figure out what to do next.

My house was quiet and dark when I got there, and for the first time since moving here, I was nervous to be alone. I grabbed a knife out of the drawer in the kitchen and slowly walked through my entire apartment. When I confirmed nobody was there, I ran back to the door, secured the deadbolt, and set the alarm.

I changed back into my PJs and sat on the floor with my Kindle, but I couldn't read with thoughts of what just had happened replaying in my mind. By the time I was tired enough to go to bed, I decided not to tell Ben. He couldn't do anything anyway since he was going back to school on Sunday. Not to mention, I didn't know if I had been followed or if my mind had been playing tricks on me tonight in the parking lot. I finally fell into a restless sleep, waking before the sun rose.

I spent the next day furniture shopping with Ben, when he finally decided to show up, looking pretty smug. He didn't even bother to ask why I left, and I was glad. I didn't ask how his night went either because I didn't want details.

We had a good time shopping for furniture, laughing uncontrollably while trying out mattresses because Ben thought rolling around and bouncing was the best way to test out its comfort. Ignoring the dirty looks from salespeople, I ordered what I needed, and Ben used his truck to haul my new bed and mattress home.

I finally had a bed—a real bed with an actual mattress. The rest of the furniture would be delivered next Saturday. Ben even stayed and set up my new bed before he had to leave, which reminded me why having a male best friend was so great. He had plans Saturday night, but I agreed to go with him to his parents on Sunday for dinner. I was happy to be spending time with people and not alone, which concerned me because I usually enjoyed being alone. I guess last night had scared me more than I thought.

Thankfully, dinner at his parents was uneventful. Besides Ben and I, the only others to show up were Jax, Kasey, Mia, and Luke. I played happily with Mia and chatted with Kasey about the furniture I found and my plans for decorating the apartment. When exhaustion finally caught up with me, I thanked everyone for dinner and promised to come back soon. Ben walked me to my car where we hugged and talked a few minutes before saying our goodbyes. Driving away, I realized I already missed them.

Chapter Fifteen

Lucy

I decided on Monday after work to talk to Jax and Brody. I hadn't slept well all weekend, so I was hoping they could give me some advice about security and, if I was lucky, a Taser. I remembered Kasey had said their company was called Elite Security, so I looked up the address, put it in my GPS, and headed that way. Their building looked like an old concrete box. Definitely not fancy. There wasn't a name on the building that I could see, so I wasn't even sure I was at the right place. I parked in the parking garage right next to it and walked over to the door. I thought I recognized Jax's truck, but I had no idea what Brody drove. I was hoping Christian wasn't there. The side door opened straight into an office with a very pretty woman at the front desk.

"Can I help you?" she asked.

"Um yes, is Jackson or Brody in?"

"Do you have an appointment?"

I sighed and looked down. I didn't even think to make an appointment. I was just about to ask her if I could make one when I heard, "Lucy, what are you doing here?"

I looked back toward a hallway and saw Brody walking toward the front office with a frown on his face.

"Hey, Brody. I'm sorry. I didn't think to make an appointment. I came by because I had a few security questions."

He looked at me with concern on his face and motioned for me to follow him while saying, "That's okay. Follow me to my office, and we can talk. Jax is back here too."

Hearing that helped me relax. I liked Brody but had never had a conversation with him. As a matter of fact, this past minute was the most I've ever heard him say. He opened a door at the end of the hall and stepped to the side, motioning for me to go in ahead of him.

"Lucy. Is everything okay?" Jax stood as soon as I entered the office. He gestured for me to sit in one of the chairs in front of the desk while he moved to stand beside it. Leaning his hip on the desk, he crossed his arms over his chest. Right then, I saw his resemblance to Christian. It was uncanny how they were all alike in such different ways. Brody stood behind the desk but continued to stare at me. A monitor on the wall showing the front office explained how they knew I was here.

"It's probably nothing," I began. "It's just that lately, I've had a feeling someone's watching me." I stopped to watch their reactions to see if they thought I was crazy.

I watched the silent exchange between the two men before Brody asked, "Why do you feel like someone's watching you?"

I sighed and tried to find the words to explain that most of the time, it's only been a gut feeling. "At first, it was only a feeling, and then when I would turn to look around or glance to the side, I always thought I saw a flash of something. I honestly thought I was being paranoid, so I ignored it. But…"

"But…?" Jax encouraged me to continue with a wave of his hand.

I paused and looked at the two brothers. "Listen, I haven't told Ben any of this yet. I mean, if or when there's something to worry about, I will tell him, but I would appreciate if we could keep this between us for now. He can be a little overprotective of me."

I didn't miss the look that passed between the brothers even though I could not interpret it.

"This stays between us—" Jax started and then put up his hand to silence me when I tried to interrupt, before emphasizing, "For now. Now tell us what's happened that brought you in now and not before."

I shifted my eyes back and forth between their faces, but their expressions remained blank, so I started, "The other night when we all met at Mac's…" I paused, and they both nodded their heads. "Well, I left by myself after I used the restroom because I…" I hesitated. "I was just ready to go. Anyway, on my way to my car, I thought I heard footsteps in the parking lot, so I looked around but as usual, saw nothing. Even so, I started walking faster, and then I heard footsteps again, and they sounded heavier and closer." I paused, lost in my memory, and rubbed my chilled arms. "I ran as fast as I could, but the footsteps got faster and louder. They sounded so close," I whispered, closing my eyes. I shook my head as if that would shake away the feeling of panic trying to take hold. "I ran out in front of a car, and he honked his horn before I even realized he was there, but it provided a barrier between whoever was following me and my car. When I made it to my car, I locked the doors and went home. I was too scared to come back in the bar for help."

Looking up, I saw both Brody and Jax looking at one another with troubled expressions.

"Anything else odd happen over the weekend?" Brody asked.

I shook my head. "No, but I wasn't alone a whole lot because Ben was home, and we spent time together."

Brody began pacing behind the desk, hands on his hips while Jax rubbed his chin, obviously in thought. Were they trying to find a way to tell me it was nothing and not make me feel crazy? This hadn't been a good idea. Honestly, what was I thinking? They couldn't do anything about a strange feeling and a one time. I didn't even know what the parking lot thing was.

"I'm sorry, guys." They both stopped and looked up. "This was silly. I'm sure it's nothing but me being paranoid. My new job takes me to some shady parts of town, and I meet some people who give me the creeps, so I'm sure this is my imagination. I realize how crazy it sounds after saying it aloud. I didn't mean to waste your time with this. I just thought maybe I could do something security-wise to feel safer. I knew the police would tell me they couldn't do anything without more to go on, so I didn't even bother Luke with this."

"You're not wasting our time," Jax stated adamantly. "But I'm not sure what we can do right now without more to go on." He looked at Brody, who nodded, and continued. "Actually, we've recently decided to bring on a friend of Brody's who specializes in tracking and investigation. We've had people come to us for help in cases like these that, up till now, we would refer out because it's not what our company was designed for. Since there's an obvious need for private investigators in this area, we've added that service on a trial basis." He shook his head. "He's not due here until next week, though." Jax walked away toward the other side of the room with his hands on his hips and head down.

"How about this." Brody looked at me seriously. "You keep track of any strange things that happen during the day and report back to me. I'll keep Striker updated." Noticing my confusion, he said, "That's our new tracker." I nodded. "In the meantime, be smart. Don't be out at night alone. Use your alarms. Lock your doors. Be vigilant. Then when Striker gets here, he can check things out for you. It'll be a good case to get his feet wet with. How does that sound?"

I looked back at Jax, who nodded in agreement. "Sounds good. But I'm thinking that until Striker gets here, everything will be fine, so you don't have to put a lot of time into this or anything."

Brody snorted. "Ben will kick my fucking ass if I don't take this seriously and something happens to you. Well, he'll try at least." He laughed. I think that was the closest thing to a joke I'd ever heard from Brody.

I was almost positive I heard Jax mumble, "Chris too," when he walked by me toward Brody, but I dismissed it quickly as wishful thinking. I stood and thanked them both for hearing me out and for the advice and promised to call with anything new. It was nice to have people I trusted so close by. I was even regretting lately that Ben and I hadn't felt more for each other than friendship, but truthfully, I think I was just falling for his family. Only one brother made me feel anything, and unfortunately, that was rejection. I was almost to the door when Jax called my name. Paused, I looked back at Jax.

"If you don't mind me asking, why is Ben so protective of you? I mean, if you two are only friends, why are you afraid to tell him?"

I'd wondered recently if Ben had shared with his family about the night that had solidified our friendship. Obviously not. I smiled softly, "Ben saved me from something a few years ago." I paused and lowered my eyes to the floor before taking a deep breath. Why was this still so hard? I looked back up. "He feels guilty about it, but it was never his fault. I think he believes protecting me now is his penance."

"That explains why you're so close," Brody said. "Intense situations can form pretty strong bonds."

I smiled and nodded, knowing these guys would understand intense situations better than most.

"I also know Ben doesn't do anything he doesn't want to do. So if he wants to protect you, it's not a penance to him," he finished.

"Thank you," I whispered before I turned and walked from the office. Smiling at the receptionist, I walked a little lighter to my car, feeling for the first time since moving away from my brother that I wasn't alone.

Like I was a part of a family.

I hadn't felt that way in a long time.

For the next few days, all was quiet. I paid attention, locked my doors, set my alarm, and figured that maybe paranoia had gotten to me.

But even being vigilant sometimes wasn't enough.

Chapter Sixteen

Lucy

Beep, beep, beep. I quickly entered the alarm code at work. Another night of hardly any sleep. No matter how well everything had been going, my mind still wouldn't allow me to sleep for longer than a few hours at a time. I figured if I couldn't sleep, I might as well get a jump on some of my paperwork. It was always strange being the first one in the office. It felt disconcerting to be in an empty building that was usually so full of noise and people.

I went into the back to the kitchen and thankfully found the coffee pot. After starting a fresh brew, I turned to go back to my desk but stopped immediately when I saw a shadow pass underneath the door to the kitchen. Okay, it's probably just someone else who came in early.

Then why wouldn't they call out that they were here? I watched the door closely until I saw the shadow again, and this time, it didn't pass by. It stopped. I backed out of the kitchen to the door that led to the alley in the back.

When the kitchen door started to open, I slammed through the back door and ran down the still dark alley. I couldn't hear anything behind me, but I kept running. I could see a light at the end of the alley where the lights from other businesses were starting to turn on.

I screamed out when a hard force hit me from behind and knocked me to the ground on my stomach. The pavement scraped into the front of my legs below my skirt. I threw my elbow back, which the attacker obviously wasn't expecting because he jerked back enough that I could pull myself up to my knees. My hands scraped along the road while I scrambled to stand. When I was up, I started running again, but only made it a few steps before I was slammed into the wall of my office building, face-first.

He pressed his body up against my back, which definitely proved this was a man because his hard-on pressed into my ass. He grabbed my wrists and threw my arms above my head before turning me around to face him. He was wearing a black ski mask, so all I could see was his brown eyes. And he was smiling. I couldn't see what his other hand was doing until I felt the cold prick of a blade against my neck.

"Scream and I'll slit your throat," he stated coldly. My breathing rasped as I looked both right and left for anyone or anything to help me. When his arms loosened their hold on my wrists a little, I instinctively kicked out my leg and hit his shin, which caused him to step back. Tightening his grip on my wrists again, he leaned down into my face, and whispered, "Keep fighting, bitch. It makes this so much better." I swallowed hard and felt tears in my eyes. His voice seemed familiar, but I couldn't place it.

Knowing I had no real chance of escape without fighting him, I continued to kick at his shins. He pulled the knife from my neck and lowered it until I couldn't see it anymore. I heard the sound of material ripping and felt a tug on my skirt. Then he smiled, right before I felt the pain of his fist hitting my cheekbone. I screamed out, and he hit me again, but harder. He grabbed my throat with his hand and pushed me into the wall when my knees buckled. I'm not sure when he let go of my wrists, but it didn't matter because he tossed me to the ground. When his boot kicked me in the side, I tried my best to roll into a ball, but I lost track of where he was after the next few blows.

Finally, he stopped and bent down, whispering, "Now we finish this."

My body shifted when he began to pick me up, which made me cry out, and he covered my mouth with his hand. Just as he was standing up with me, he dropped me down to the ground and ran away. That was when I heard someone yell, "Call 911!" I drifted in and out of consciousness, only hearing parts of what was said to me. I didn't answer, but tears formed in the corners of my eyes when sirens blared in the small alley.

"Open your eyes." Warm hands settled on either side of my face as a man's voice spoke gently to me. "Can you hear me?"

I opened my eyes enough to see Luke hovering over me and shouting to the paramedic kneeling beside me. Luke was pushed aside when another paramedic kneeled on the other side of me, calling for a stretcher. I couldn't understand what they were saying after that, and before long, I heard nothing at all.

Chapter Seventeen

Christian

"This better be fucking important," I mumbled into the phone while looking at the clock that told me it wasn't even seven yet, and I'd only gone to bed around three.

"You need to get to the hospital right now!"

That made me sit up. "Why? What the hell's going on?"

"Fuck, man, I don't want to tell you over the phone. Just get dressed and meet me there." I finally recognized Luke's voice before he disconnected. I jumped out of bed, threw on some clothes, and grabbed my keys before running out the door.

It took about fifteen minutes from my place to get to the hospital. Shit, I didn't even know where I was going. Moving quickly toward the emergency room, I figured that was the best place to start. I stopped when I saw nearly all of my family members standing near the front desk. Luke looked up, and his face dropped as I approached. He stepped forward while the rest of the family stood back but still faced us. I felt the presence of my brothers creating a wall of support. That was how it always was when one of us was being singled out. The others literally had our back.

"What the hell is going on, Luke?" I growled anxiously.

I watched Luke swallow and then rub the back of his neck. "I was called out this morning to a scene that resembled the ones I've been investigating." He paused. "I can't tell you much, but we have an open investigation on a serial rapist."

"Okay, and…?" I was losing my patience. Why the hell does this involve me and the rest of the family?

When someone approach from my side, I turned to face Jax. "It's Lucy, man. She was found in the alley this morning behind her office building."

My stomach dropped.

Lucy.

Then I remembered what Luke said about his investigation. "Are you telling me she was raped?"

I watched Luke look toward Jax grimly. "We don't know. The doctor's with her now."

"What made them think she had been? Enough that they called you?"

Luke hesitated.

"Tell me exactly what happened, and why the hell everyone is here!" I had to know everything.

"We're here, son, because Lucy doesn't have any family, and when Luke called to tell me, I felt she was going to need all the support she could get," my dad stated calmly.

I heard Luke let out a long breath. "She was found this morning by the maintenance man of the building who was clocking in. Said he heard some scuffling around behind the building, and when he walked back there, he saw a man picking Lucy up off the ground. He called out, which caused the man to drop her and run. That's when the police were called. We don't have any other details yet."

"But you were on the scene?" I asked.

Luke nodded. "Not initially, but the officers have been told that anytime a woman is found beaten and possibly raped, I'm to be called. The responding officer called me immediately when he saw her skirt was torn and she had blood on her legs. I got there right about the same time as the paramedics. She opened her eyes only briefly before she was put in the ambulance."

I started pacing. It was as if my body was exploding out of my skin and couldn't be still. Luke knew about me and Lucy. He was the only one I'd told, but it seemed like everyone knew now. Looking up at my brothers, I realized Ben wasn't here, which made me happy. How much of a prick did that make me? I'd been waiting for them to decide they wanted to be together, but I wanted to see her before he came, and I lost her forever. I was afraid this would be the moment he got his head out of his ass and admitted he's had feelings for her. These past few months have been torture. Trying to avoid seeing her so I wouldn't do something stupid and admit my own feelings for her. The truth was, I knew the first time I saw her that I wanted her for myself, but she was never mine. She belonged to Ben, and I shouldn't have been there. I should've left, but I couldn't. I needed to see for myself that she was okay.

It felt like hours went by before I heard a nurse call Luke to the front desk. I walked over to stand with my family while Luke and the nurse whispered quietly.

Finally, he made his way over to us. "She was just taken to surgery. The nurse isn't permitted to disclose information, but she did say that her shoulder needs to be set."

"That's it? That's all the information she has?" I spit out.

"We're lucky she told us that much. Now we have to wait for the doctor," he answered patiently.

We waited and watched as others came and went from the emergency room. All came after Lucy and left before there was any news. It felt like days but was only, in fact, hours. We drank coffee Mom and Dad bought from the cafeteria. It was awful, but at least it was something.

"Where is she?" Ben yelled when he ran by me toward Luke. Luke looked at me with a grim expression, probably realizing what I'd always known. That today Ben would no longer be able to deny his feelings.

"Doctor hasn't come out yet." Luke spoke quietly.

"What the hell happened?"

I listened while Luke replayed the same story for Ben that he had told all of us already. "Now what?"

"Now, we wait," Luke answered.

Ben seemed as forlorn as the rest of the family and found his spot in the waiting room to linger. Looking around the room, one would assume that Lucy was family, and truthfully, she felt like family. She had since the first time Ben brought her home only a short time back. Sometimes, when you meet someone, you have the feeling they were always supposed to be in your life, and that was how Lucy felt to me.

"Who's here for Lucy Reynolds?" The doctor interrupted my thoughts, and I, along with all of my family, started toward him. Luke held up his hand, probably realizing we were all about to lie in some way to the doctor to prove we were her family. "I'm the detective on this case. Unfortunately, her brother isn't here yet."

The doctor and Luke walked away and began quietly talking while we stood waiting.

"I called Landon," Ben announced and then looked around, probably seeing the confusion. "Her brother."

"What about her parents?" Mom asked.

"I'll leave that up to Landon when he gets here. I only have his number, not her parents. He's on his way, but he was out of the country and has to finish with a stunt set he was working on. I'm supposed to call him as soon as I have more information," Ben said.

"Why the fuck wouldn't he leave now?" Ben turned toward me when I spoke, but his eyes traveled over my shoulder, and I knew Luke must be coming based on his anxious expression. I quickly turned to face him.

Luke came to stop right before us. "Well, the good news is she's stable and in recovery." He held up his hand to silence our questions. "And there is no evidence of rape."

"Oh, thank god!" Mom exclaimed, voicing our thoughts judging by the relief on everyone's faces.

"But...?" Dad inquired.

Luke looked forlorn. "She has extensive injuries."

"Just tell us straight out," I demanded impatiently.

My brothers nodded in agreement.

Luke took a deep breath. "She was beaten badly. Doc says she has a concussion, three broken ribs, and bruises covering much of her body. They had to reset her shoulder, which was dislocated." He paused. "He said she's unconscious right now, but that doesn't concern him."

"Why not?" Jake inquired.

"Apparently in these situations, he is not initially concerned because it will give her body time to heal. However, he will become concerned if she stays unresponsive for more than twenty-four hours. They're putting her in a room now."

"Can we see her?" I asked.

Luke gave me a sad smile and shook his head. "Only I'm allowed right now, and then when Landon gets here, he can approve anyone else."

"Do you think it's your guy?" Jax spoke up.

"Not sure. He fits the description, but he wasn't as discreet as he's been up until now. He would have been desperate to attempt to snatch her where he did. I'll need more information from Lucy before I decide if this is related to my case."

"I updated Landon. He'll be on a flight out soon, but in the meantime, he'll call the nurses' desk and ask them to allow us in to see her until he can get here." Ben interrupted. "He'll also call their parents."

That was a relief, and hopefully, Landon could get us in because she shouldn't be alone right now.

Thinking back to Luke's comments, I inquired, "So you're saying there's a chance this could have been random?"

I didn't miss the look that passed between Jax and Luke, and obviously Ben hadn't either because he looked directly at Jax. "What?"

Brody came forward and stood beside Jax. Christ, I forgot he was even here. He was so damn quiet, always had been, but that seemed worse lately. "It's not random."

"How would you know that?" Ben asked.

With his hands on his hips, Brody let out a loud exhale. "Lucy came to us earlier this week and told us she felt like she was being followed."

What the fuck? She asked for help and still ended up hurt. Feeling like my blood was boiling, I turned to Brody and growled, "She came to you for help, and she's still lying in a fucking hospital bed?"

Brody narrowed his eyes, and growled back, "We planned to have Striker on it when he got here next week. She had nothing concrete, only a feeling, except for one instance, and in the meantime, we walked her through safety precautions."

Ben shook his head. "What instance?"

Brody didn't move his eyes from mine when he answered. "She thought she was chased the night we all met at Mac's." He leaned forward. "For some reason, she left in a hurry and didn't check her surroundings. Said she just needed to leave." He grunted. "You wouldn't know anything about that, would you, Chris?"

I didn't think; only reacted. Of all my faults, that was probably the worst one. I grabbed Brody by the front of his shirt and pushed him until we reached the wall. Slamming him into the wall, I got up in his face, and we stared at each other, breathing heavily. I could hear my brothers behind us, preparing to break up the ensuing fight.

"Why don't you say what you mean, man?"

Brody grabbed my shirt front and flipped our positions until my back was against the wall and lowered his voice. "Maybe if you'd man up, Lucy wouldn't be at work at five in the morning when her start time is eight. Maybe she'd be at home busy with you."

He pushed me harder into the wall. "I've been watching every step she's taken since we talked, but I had no idea she would drag herself out of bed and be at work three hours early. The way I see it, man, we both dropped the fucking ball on this."

He loosened his hold on my shirt, then backed up with his hands in the air. The signature move to show that as far as he was concerned, the fight was over. Putting my hands on my hips, I sidestepped my brothers, never making eye contact with Ben, and walked outside.

Chapter Eighteen

Christian

I was sitting on the bench outside the emergency room entrance, head down, hands on the back of my neck when I felt someone settle in beside me. Not even bothering to look up, I knew it was my dad. He's always stepped aside with us boys, letting us wade through problems on our own without inserting himself until he felt we'd reached our limit.

He laid his hand on my back. "I've been watching you with our Lucy. Always suspected something." I snorted. Our Lucy. He had no idea how much I wanted that to be true. "Way I see it, your brother doesn't claim her, maybe it's time you do."

I shook my head and sat back against the bench. "We both know that's about to change. Besides, she belongs to Ben. Always has."

"Never known you to back down from anything before."

I faced him. "This is different. Pop. You've got to see that. I've never been with the same girl as any of the boys. None of us has. It's what you do for your brothers. You, of all people, should get that. You have brothers."

He nodded. "Yep, that's true. But I have it on good authority they've never had that kind of relationship."

I had no idea how he knew that. "And you don't think it's unusual how close they are?"

He leaned toward me. "You find out why that is, my boy." He patted my leg before standing and looking down at me. "And I'll bet you'll realize how much time you've wasted. Now let's go. Lucy needs us."

I followed him through the sliding doors just as Luke turned away from the front desk. "They have her in a room. Landon called in and gave permission for us to be in there with her, but the doctor gave orders of no more than two at a time. I need to go in and see if she's awake yet to give me any details she might remember."

We all hustled to find her room and found a waiting room close by for those of us not in with her. We were lucky that right now we were the only family there. We don't leave a whole lot of room for anyone else.

"I'm going in with you." Ben spoke directly to Luke.

Luke glanced my way, but seeing I wasn't going to disagree, he nodded, and they left. The room was silent. Jax quietly spoke on the phone to Kasey, giving her updates. I didn't realize she and Lucy had become close, but apparently, they had if his side of the conversation was anything to go by. He asked Mom if she would go to Mia after seeing Lucy so that Kasey could come in. They were allowing only short visits right now, so we didn't have to wait long for Ben and Luke to come back to the waiting room. We all stood when they stopped in the doorway.

Ben shook his head and sat, putting his head down and in his hands. We looked at Luke. These situations weren't new to him in the line of work he was in, so he obviously was more equipped for them, but even he looked shaken.

"I want to warn you…" He paused, shaking his head. "She doesn't look good. There's a lot of swelling and bruising." His jaw tightened, and he gritted his teeth before releasing it, and saying, "Just be ready when you go in."

I waited and watched as everyone took their turns in pairs. Mom and Dad decided they would be first so Mom could go to be with Mia. She was crying softly when she came out, and Dad has his arm protectively around her. He said he would drive her to stay with Mia and bring Kasey back. Next, Jax and Brody went in. You could read the guilt on their faces before they went in, but when they came out, those looks had changed to anger. They announced they had to leave, and as they were walking by my chair, Brody stopped.

Leaning down somewhat, he whispered in a lethal tone, "I'm going to find this bastard."

At some point, Julie had arrived. I didn't expect that, but she did, and she went in with Jake. He honestly seemed to be trying to make some kind of relationship with her, considering she was pregnant. I realized Ben and I were the only ones still there besides Luke, and he still had his head down.

Leaning my head against the wall, I tried to be patient. I was going in next. I could've gone before, but I wanted to be alone when I went in. Jake looked pissed when they came back out, but I wasn't surprised. They had become friends over the past few months. He had made sure to keep an eye out for her and help her with things while she got settled. He met my eyes briefly, shaking his head, before he went to Ben and patted him on the shoulder. He got up and walked out with them into the hallway. I looked around and realized I was the only one left to go.

"You want me to come with you?" Luke asked from across the room.

I turned toward him and shook my head. "No. I was waiting to go in by myself."

"That's what I figured. Stay as long as you need. I'll run interference out here." And he would. Luke was probably the one most like our dad. Always there, no questions asked, no judgment.

I nodded. "Thanks."

I turned and walked to her room, only to pause outside with my hand on the handle. God, I wished Cam were here right now. I needed him. I could've talked to him. I couldn't think about that right now, or I wasn't going to get through this, so I pushed the door open.

I'd expected her to look bad, but I hadn't realized how badly beaten she was. I grabbed the back of the chair nearest to her bed when my legs buckled. Using it to hold on, I inched closer until I stood by the side and began looking around. There were tubes and wires everywhere, and a machine was beeping. Her eyes were closed, but I could tell that even if she wasn't asleep, they still would be. They were that swollen. She had a collection of nasty bruises on her face and arms. Everywhere I could see was already bruising. I sat down and took her hand in mine, silently begging her to open her eyes.

When she didn't, I leaned forward and whispered, my voice thick with emotion, "I'm sorry, baby, so sorry. For everything. You need to wake up so I can tell you that. I don't care anymore about the right thing to do. When you get out of here, I'm making you mine." I paused and leaned my forehead down to her hand. "I don't care what I have to do to make that happen."

I realized at that moment, seeing her like this, I would do anything to bring us together. This could've turned out so differently, and I would've regretted my choices for the rest of my life.

I was taking control now, and I didn't care who I had to go through to do that.

Chapter Nineteen

Lucy

I woke to the sound of beeping and something heavy on my arm. Slowly opening my eyes, I looked around, feeling confused as to where I was. I hurt. Everything hurt. My mouth felt dry, so dry that when I tried to swallow, there was nothing to swallow. What the hell was beeping? Blinking slowly, I looked toward the machine where the beeping sound was coming from and followed the cords down to something on my finger. I noticed the IV in my hand and followed the line up to the machine with the bag slowly dripping. The hospital. Why was I in the hospital?

Looking back down, I saw the bruises on my arms, and suddenly, I had a flashback of a dark alley and being pinned to the wall. I jerked forward, trying to sit up, but fell back when a pain crashed through my shoulder. I closed my eyes and tried to control my breathing. When the sharp pain subsided, I opened my eyes again and looked at my right arm, wondering what feels heavy against it. I looked down to see a large body sitting in the chair beside my bed with his head down, cheek resting against my right hand. Hearing the door to my room open, I looked up to see a nurse walking in.

When she saw me looking back at her, she smiled. "You're awake. We were really starting to worry about you," she said pleasantly while walking around to stand by the side of the bed. "How are you feeling? Do you have any pain?"

I shook my head and opened my mouth to answer when the head on my arm jerked up and looked right at me. Christian.

"You're awake." He jumped from his seat and turned to the nurse. "Shouldn't you get the doctor?"

She smiled patiently. "I plan to. I was checking on Ms. Reynolds' pain first."

"You're in pain?" He leaned in and took my hand.

I tried to answer, but my throat was so dry that it felt covered in sandpaper. I tried to swallow and start again, but my words came out hoarse and on a whisper.

"Here, let's give you a few sips of water. That should make it a little easier to talk." The nurse poured water in a cup and offered me a few small sips from a straw. "Do you want to try again?"

I nodded. "Pain," I said, in a small breathy voice. "In my shoulder." I took the cup from her and took a few more sips of water while glancing at Christian in confusion.

"Okay, honey. I'm going to go page the doctor now, and we'll see what he wants to do." She looked between Christian and me. "You sure are lucky with this one. He hasn't left your side since you were brought in."

I broke my stare from Christian and looked at the nurse, who smiled and nodded before she left my room.

"Can I get you anything?" I looked back at Christian, who was watching me closely. He looked rumpled, like he hadn't changed his clothes in a while. And tired. The large gray circles under his eyes announcing his lack of sleep.

"What are you doing here?" I whispered before lifting my cup and taking another sip. He sat back down and leaned forward, relief evident on his face.

"I've been waiting for you to come back to me." He took the

cup from my hand and put it on the tray. Then he took my hand in his. Feeling confused, I looked around the room at anywhere but him. I didn't understand what he was saying to me. It must be the pain meds fogging my brain.

"Hey," he said quietly, "look at me."

I rolled my head back toward him and flinched in pain. Even just moving my head hurt.

"Are you in that much pain?" When I nodded slightly, he looked back toward the door and asked impatiently, "Where is the fucking doctor?"

I looked at the door too, hoping the doctor would come in and talk to me about this pain, especially in my shoulder. Anticipating a doctor, I was surprised when the door opened, and Jack came in. Smiling big, he came to the bed and pushed Christian out of his way before leaning down and kissing me on the cheek.

"Welcome back." He smirked at a pissed off Christian.

I smiled and responded in a raspy voice, "Thanks."

He straightened and stepped back, rubbing his hands together. "I called Anna, who will call the rest of the family to let them know you're awake now. Ben and Landon are close by and should be here any minute."

"My brother's here?" I inquired, quietly.

"Sure is, sweetheart."

"Pop, how the hell did you know she was awake?" Christian asked.

"I was in the waiting room and heard the nurse page the doctor," he answered.

He barely finished saying that, and the door was pushed open quickly by Landon, followed by Ben. They pushed their way to me.

"Holy fuck, you scared me," Landon admitted. "How are you feeling?" I looked up to see both of them staring down at me with concerned expressions.

I opened my mouth to answer, but my throat wasn't cooperating again. Letting my eyes wander to the side, I spotted

Christian who moved toward me and then grabbed the cup of water that I couldn't reach.

He held it up for me to sip. "Good?" he whispered when I let go of the straw.

"I'm okay," I answered softly. "Just pain in my shoulder."

"Ms. Reynolds. It's nice to see you awake."

I looked over Landon's shoulder to see a doctor coming into my room. He cleared the room quickly, only asking if I wanted anyone to stay. I looked around the room at the four sets of eyes staring back at me. How could I choose? Landon was my brother. He should by rights be who I chose, but Ben's been my best friend and protector for a long time now. I didn't know what Christian was to me, but I knew I felt better when he was near. And Jack. Jack was how I wish my father was.

He must have sensed my indecision because he took the lead. "Okay, boys, let's go wait in the waiting room for the rest of the family. We'll leave Lucy and Landon with the doctor."

I couldn't meet Ben and Christian's eyes, so I kept mine on Jack. I smiled a small smile, and he nodded and winked back.

The doctor took the time to tell me more about my injuries. He explained that my shoulder was dislocated, so they operated. I would need to be in a sling for at least six weeks and do physical therapy, but the pain should subside soon. He also explained he couldn't do much for my ribs except pain management until they healed. And they would heal slowly, according to him. Since everything else was healing well, he said they would monitor me for the day and possibly send me home tomorrow. He also said he would be in tomorrow morning to discuss aftercare at home if I was discharged. He then had the nurse put something in my IV that he promised would help with the pain.

After he left, Landon sat in the seat beside my bed and held my hand. "I called Mom and Dad. They're in London at a conference." He lowered his eyes.

"They're not coming, are they?" I surmised.

He shook his head. "Sorry, sis. When I called on the way here to tell them you were awake, they decided to stay until the end. They promised to come see you when they're back in the States."

"How thoughtful of them," I responded sarcastically, making Landon chuckle.

"Can I come in?" I looked to see Luke standing in the doorway.

I nodded, and he walked the rest of the way in. "How are you feeling, Luce?"

"Okay." I smiled softly.

"You feel like answering some questions?" Luke asked.

Realizing he was here in a professional capacity, I said quietly, "I don't have a choice, do I?"

Frowning, he ran his hand across the back of his neck before saying, "You have no idea how much I don't want you to have to relive this, but the truth is, there were no witnesses. I have nothing to go on except the information you can give me."

I nodded because I understood that, but it didn't make me want to remember it.

"So, can you tell me what you remember?"

I looked toward Landon, who nodded and then said in a voice a little above a whisper, "I don't remember much. It's almost like there are little pieces of a puzzle in my mind, but I can't put it together."

"That's okay, Lucy. Can you give me those little pieces? I may be able to help you put them in place."

I nodded. "I know I went to work early, and I remember disarming the alarm. I think I was in the kitchen when I heard a noise…" I paused and closed my eyes, trying to make the images clearer. "I'm not sure what happened, but I know I was running down the alley when someone pushed me down from behind. Everything after that are moments I remember."

I looked at Luke. "What do you mean, moments?"

I shook my head, trying to find the right words to describe what my mind was allowing. "Like I remember being against the wall with his hand around my wrists. And I remember hearing my skirt tear." I closed my eyes, lost in the memories. "I remember the feeling of a cold knife blade against my throat. Then I was on the ground, and my side was burning, but..." I opened my eyes when a tear escaped from the corner of my eye, and I shook my head. "But I can't remember how it all happened."

Landon came to my side then from his spot at the foot of the bed and took my hand. "You're doing great, Luce," he said supportively.

"You are doing great," Luke reiterated. "And don't worry about putting it all in place. Every little detail you can give me is helpful. Sometimes, it's the little pieces of information that give me the best leads."

I shook my head. "What do you mean?"

"Well, for example, any tattoos or piercings? Hair color, eye color? Anything that seemed odd or particular about him?"

"Okay, well, he was wearing a black ski mask, I remember that."

"That's good. Anything else?"

Landon squeezed my hand, and I quietly thanked god he came home. "His eyes were brown. I only had the chance to see that when he turned his head to the entrance of the alley. It was still a little dark that early," I explained.

Luke nodded, his eyes searching mine.

"I don't think..." I stopped. Shaking my head side to side, I was frustrated because I wasn't giving him anything helpful when it came back to me. "Wait."

"What?" Luke leaned forward. "What do you remember?"

I pulled myself up a little more in the bed. "His voice."

"What about his voice, Lucy?"

I looked over at Luke with wide eyes. "I remember thinking I recognized his voice."

"You think it was someone you knew?" Landon pressed, with even more concern in his voice now.

I looked at Landon and nodded my head. "Yeah, I remember thinking something was so familiar about him."

"This is really good, Lucy. We can narrow it down a lot if we concentrate on people in your circle. Ones you've come in contact with and might want to hurt you," Luke explained. "Can you think of anyone who fits that description?"

"Who would want to hurt you, Lucy?" Landon asked.

"I don't know. I can't think of anyone right now." I felt myself getting groggy. "I think whatever the nurse gave me is making me tired."

"That's okay, Luce. You gave me a great place to start. You rest, and if you remember anything else when you wake up, give me a call. Okay?"

I nodded my head, but my eyes wouldn't stay open any longer. Right before I gave in to the peace of sleep, I thought I heard, "Who the fuck would want to hurt Lucy?" And then the quiet enveloped me.

Chapter Twenty

Lucy

It was another full day before the doctor agreed to discharge me. Because of the pain in my shoulder, he decided to keep me there to evaluate it. After deciding to try a different pain medication, I finally got some relief. I was told by the nurse that I'd had a lot of visitors, but the initial medication had made me so groggy that I was having trouble remembering.

The nurse came in with the doctor to talk to me fairly early. They gave me some aftercare information and guidelines for my shoulder, which included physical therapy. While the nurse finished taking out my IV, I heard arguing outside my door. Looking at me curiously, the nurse quickly finished up and told me I was free to get dressed and she would be back with my discharge papers. The door was pushed open, and a very angry Landon came in first, followed by Christian and then Ben, who was shaking his head. The nurse gave me a small smile, and I shrugged at her before she left.

"No, you're not!" Landon yelled at Christian.

Christian didn't even respond, bypassing Landon altogether as he approached my bed. "How are you feeling?"

I looked toward the foot of the bed at Ben and Landon, who were both staring my way.

"Okay, but I'm ready to leave," I admitted.

"That's something we need to talk to you about," Ben said.

Looking among the three men, the tension in the room increased with that one sentence. "Why? What do you mean?"

"You can't go home alone, and we're deciding who's going to stay with you," Ben said.

"What?" I asked, confused. "Of course I'm going home alone."

"You can't," Landon stated. "You're going to need help with things right now and there's the small problem of the bastard who attacked you still running loose," he said sarcastically while staring at Christian.

"Are you fucking kidding me right now?" Christian said angrily, taking a step toward Landon.

"Wait. Can someone please tell me in full sentences," I stressed, already anticipating the caveman version. "What the hell is going on?"

Landon walked the few steps to stand at the foot of my bed and curled his hands around the top of the footboard. "We all agree someone needs to stay with you for now, Luce. We're just having trouble on agreeing who that is."

I shook my head as if understanding their dilemma. "Oh, well, I can help with that." I glanced at Ben, who was smirking and shaking his head. He knew me so well. "None of you are staying with me." I held up my hand when they started talking at once, "I'm a grown woman who can take care of herself. I do not need a babysitter. Besides, the police are involved, and I'm sure they will do what they can to protect me."

"You are not fucking staying alone!" Landon exclaimed, gripping the edge of the bed.

"Lucy," Ben called my name. I looked at him and smiled. Ben was always the calm in the storm. He was also reasonable and knew all too well I would hate having a roommate, let alone a babysitter.

"Someone is going to stay with you." Wait, what? That was not what he was supposed to say. "Whether you realize it or not, you're not safe. Not at least until we catch this guy. Even Luke thinks it's safer to have someone with you." He added the last part, knowing I would take it seriously that the police felt I was unsafe, and it wasn't only these three exaggerating. "The only thing you need to decide is who you're comfortable having stay at your place with you."

"You're going back to school, Ben," Christian said seriously.

"I'm not going back until I know Lucy is safe."

"That's what the rest of us are here to make sure of."

"Ben." I interrupted. "You have to go back to school. Why would you even consider not going back?"

"You know why." He frowned, meeting my eyes.

Shaking my head, I said, "Ben—".

"What the hell does that mean?" Christian growled, glaring at Ben.

"That means that Lucy's safety is the most important thing," Ben stated.

Christian walked to Ben until they were face-to-face, "Are you sure this isn't something else, little brother?"

Ben stood straighter, looking directly into Christian's eyes, and said in a low voice, "If this was something else, you wouldn't even be in this room."

Recognizing that tone in Ben's voice, I interrupted. "Okay, you two. That's enough. I think this is ridiculous, but if someone is going to insist on staying with me, I guess I have no choice. But Ben, you need to go back to school." Ben turned so his entire body was toward me. "Come here." I motioned for him to come to my side and held out my hand. He walked to the side of the bed with the saddest look on his face and took my hand in his. "I need you to stop this. You are not my personal bodyguard. You are not solely responsible for my safety. And you are NOT," I stressed, "responsible for the past. I made my own decisions then, and I make my own decisions now." I paused and then smiled up at him.

"You're my best friend, and I love you, but you need to go back to school, okay? This can't be the reason you don't finish what you've worked so hard for."

He shook his head while squeezing my hand. "And you'll let one of these idiots stay with you?"

I sighed and looked past him at Landon and Christian, my brother and my weakness competing over who gets to stay with me. How could I ever choose between these two men?

"Landon, what about your job?" I asked.

He leaned in. "The last one was finishing up when I got the call about you, so I'm officially on leave until I say otherwise. Besides, I told you before that I was thinking about doing something else. This is as good a time as any to start working on that."

"I don't want you making a life decision because of some guilt over me."

He sighed, standing up straight and rubbing the back of his neck with his hand. He looked at me seriously. "Lucy, I've been thinking about this for a while now. This just forced me to look at things in my life and realize I want to spend more time with my sister and have time for friends again."

I nodded. I could understand that. Lately, Landon and I had both been guilty of putting our aspirations ahead of everything else, including each other and friends. I was starting to feel more like our parents than I cared to.

"Listen, that's great. I think you should spend time together, but the fact remains that I am more qualified to keep her safe. My job is in security in case you forgot," Christian said to Landon.

"If you're so qualified, then why the hell are we all standing in a fucking hospital room deciding who will stay with her?" Landon sneered.

"What did you just say?" Christian growled.

"I'm her brother. I'm the one who's staying with her," Landon snapped. "I don't even know why we're having this conversation."

You could feel the tension crackling in the room. I noticed Christian's jaw was clenched, and his hands were hanging at his sides in fists.

"Yeah, well I'm the one she's fucking," Christian replied angrily.

"Christian!" I shouted, feeling my face get hot. I couldn't believe he said that, especially in front of my brother and Ben. Oh crap, Ben. Like there wasn't already enough tension between those two. "What the hell is wrong with you?"

Landon turned his body back to face me completely with a stunned expression. "Is that true? Are you in some kind of relationship with this guy?"

"No," I answered quickly and shook my head while looking at Christian. "I am absolutely not in a relationship with him."

"Yet." The bastard smirked. He actually smirked, and I narrowed my eyes.

"Ever," I hissed.

"Are we interrupting?" I heard from the door.

Breaking my stare with Christian, I looked toward the voice only to see Jax and Brody. Jeez, how many people could fit in this room? Wasn't there a limit on how many visitors at one time or something?

Feeling frustrated and pissed off, I said adamantly, "You know what? I would like everyone to leave right now so I can get dressed." Then realizing how ungrateful I must sound when everyone was here only to help me, I softened my voice, "Please."

"No," Christian said.

"No?" I repeated surprised. "What the hell do you mean, no?"

He leaned down until he was right in my face, lips close to mine. I swallowed hard and backed my head even farther into the pillow, which made him grin before saying, "How are you going to dress yourself with your arm in a sling and broken ribs?"

He raised his eyebrows and stared into my eyes before he backed away and stood tall again. Looking around the room, I saw five sets of eyes watching me all with different expressions on their faces ranging from anger to full-blown smiles.

Jerks.

I smiled sweetly at Christian, hoping he assumed I was going to ask him for help before I grabbed the call button for the nurse. "Problem solved." I pushed the button. "Now you can go." I heard chuckling on the other side of me and turned my head quickly to stare down Ben who, after seeing the look on my face, tried to stop smiling but failed miserably.

"Okay, everyone out." A very small nurse I heard before I saw came bounding into the room. "My goodness girl, how many boys you got after you? You know what you need? You need a girlfriend to help sort through them. Everyone needs their girls." She said without taking a breath.

"Tell me about it," I mumbled.

"We'll wait outside, Luce," Ben said.

I nodded and looked at Landon who shook his head and while rubbing the back of his neck, walked to the door.

The nurse continued shooing everyone out until she got to Christian. He looked down at me before he walked away, and lowered his voice, "I'll be waiting outside this room until you're changed. And then I'm going to take you home." He grinned right at the nurse before he pushed through the door.

"Woo, girl," she muttered, watching him leave. After he left, she turned and looked at me. "You want some advice?"

"Sure, why not," I answered on a sigh.

She laughed. "I've seen a lot in my life, especially inside the walls of this hospital. And you know what I can say for certain?"

I shook my head because I had no idea where she was going with this.

"People will come and go in your life. Some will be good for you. Some bad. Although…" She winked at me and snickered. "Sometimes the bad ones are very good." I smiled, and then she became more serious. "A lot will come and go. Some will even stay a while.

But the ones who come when things are good and stay when things get bad are the ones who matter." I nodded while she leaned over the side of the bed, and with a hand on my back, she helped me to sit and then stand. She turned me to face her and put her hands on my biceps. "That boy you're trying so hard to push away has been here while things were bad. He never left. In my book, that means something."

I nodded because it did in my book too.

I just didn't know what that was yet.

Chapter Twenty-one

Christian

Walking back into the waiting room, I braced for the impending fight. Meeting Ben's gaze first, I realized this conversation was a long time coming, and I couldn't avoid it any longer. I walked right to him, seeing in my periphery that Landon was coming toward us, as were Jax and Brody. Might as well deal with them all at once.

Looking Ben in the eye because he deserved that respect, I asked the question I should've asked months ago. "Do you want more with her?"

He raised his eyebrow. "More than what?"

He was going to make me say it, but I should've known he would. He always was a little bastard.

"More than friends." I growled. "You know what I'm asking, fucker."

"Seems to me, from what I heard in there, that what I want hasn't mattered," he answered sarcastically.

Who the fuck did he think he was? All those fucking months of guilt over wanting my brother's girl until I couldn't stay away any more. Then the memory of having her and walking out rushed over me, and I snapped. Moving quickly until I was right in his face,

I grabbed a bunch of his shirt in my fist. Jax moved to stand behind my back while Brody and Landon flanked Ben.

"Now boys, we all know this has been coming, but don't forget where we are and who's coming out of that room in a few minutes," Jax said.

Ignoring Jax's warning, I responded with quiet intensity, "If what you wanted didn't matter, asshole, I would've had her the first day you brought her home. I held off, waiting for you to move in, but you haven't, so I'm thinking now that you either don't want her or you don't deserve her."

"Neither one of us deserves her," Ben answered quickly.

I met his eyes and gave him a chin lift in acknowledgment because he was right. Neither one of us did deserve her, but I was too selfish to care anymore.

"Lucy and I are best friends," he admitted, "but that's all we'll ever be. She's like a sister to me. We were honest about that."

That was all I needed as my green light to move forward, but then I remembered something.

"What was she talking about in there when she said you shouldn't feel guilty?" I loosened my grip on his shirt and backed up a little.

Ben shook his head and closed his eyes for a minute. When he opened them up, I saw a mixture of pain and guilt swimming in their depths. "That's her story to tell, man. I won't betray her confidence by telling you, but know it was bad, and that I didn't protect her."

"I don't believe that, brother, but we'll let it go for now." Brody spoke up.

I let go of Ben's shirt, still trying to absorb what he'd said, and turned my attention to Landon. "We need to figure this out, man, because I'm not going anywhere. And I have every intention of taking her home. And staying."

Landon put his hands on his hips and backed up a little, obviously needing space.

"We can't ask her to decide between us because she won't. She would toss us both out on our asses instead." Landon smirked and nodded in agreement.

"I'm not leaving town." He walked closer to me and looked in my eyes. "I'm going to let you stay with her, but just know that I'll be watching every move you make." He paused. "And if I think for one minute that you're not protecting her the way you should, *you* will be the one who needs protection."

I hadn't even realized I'd moved forward until Jax's hand slapped against my chest to hold me back.

He leaned forward, and whispered in my ear, "You would do the same for Grace."

That stopped me because he was right. I would do anything to protect Grace. We all would.

So I nodded at Landon and bit back the overwhelming urge to tell him to go fuck himself.

Chapter Twenty-two

Lucy

I hated this.

I hated this sling. I hated that my ribs hurt. I hated that I was being a bitch.

But more than anything, I hated that I needed help.

Especially from him.

I'd never considered that guilt, or pity, or whatever we were calling it, would be the reasons he'd be in my place again. I'd been proud of myself when I finally found the nerve and my voice and told him no, but now I was standing in my living room while he took off the coat he had slung over my shoulders. I hadn't showered in almost four days, and I had no clue how I was supposed to do that alone. I was tired, grouchy, stinky, and had recently learned I was a horrible patient.

When I had walked out of my hospital room today, I was not surprised to find the same five men waiting for me, but I was surprised the tension had gone. As a matter of fact, they seemed almost friendly with one another, including Landon and Christian. I was immediately suspicious. Finding out that Christian had won the argument and was planning to stay with me wasn't surprising. Why he was insisting on all of this was bothering me. I guess if

I wanted those answers, I would need to ask him those questions.

I made my way over to the couch and sat down, already feeling tired. Damn pain pills. I heard Christian moving around behind me but didn't have the energy to look at what he was doing. We also hadn't really spoken since we left the hospital. However, most of that was my fault.

"Are there any leads on my case?" I felt like this was a good way to start a conversation. When I didn't hear anything, I turned to look over my shoulder only to see him frowning.

"No." He walked toward the couch and sat down beside me. "We haven't. Have you remembered anything else?"

I shook my head. "No."

Silence.

It seemed unless we were arguing, we had nothing to talk about. I looked down at my hands, fiddling with the edge of my shirt.

"This isn't going to work," I said before looking back up at him.

I watched as his lips tipped up in a grin. "I wondered how long it would take you to say that."

I tilted my head and glared at him. "You think you know me so well."

"Yeah, I think I do."

"Really, so what am I thinking right now?"

He leaned in until all I could concentrate on were his eyes. "Right now, you're trying to figure out how to keep me at a distance. Just far enough away that you won't be tempted."

"Oh, please." I huffed. "You think way too much of yourself."

He smiled but didn't move back. Feeling frustrated now and knowing there was no way I could have a conversation with him this close, I asked, "What the hell are you doing here, anyway?"

He shook his head. "I don't think we're going to have this conversation right now."

"Why the hell not?"

He watched me closely. "Because you don't seem to be in the right frame of mind.

"Oh, yeah. What frame of mind do I seem to be in?"

He lifted his hand to my shoulder and slowly ran the tip of his finger down my arm, so close to my body that his knuckles brushed along the outside of my breast, to my wrist. I swallowed hard and cursed the goose bumps that followed the line of his fingertip.

He reached down and took my hand in his before looking back up at me and saying quietly, "The kind where we both lose."

Lose? Lose what?

I was suddenly too tired to care, so I pulled my hand from his and with some extra effort, stood from my seat.

"I'm going to shower," I said stiffly, "and then I'm going to sleep." I walked away, then turned back to state loudly, "And I'm doing it myself." I gritted my teeth when I heard him chuckling behind me.

Showering proved to be as difficult as I thought it would be. Trying to keep my arm tight against me and not get the bandage wet, all while still trying to bathe one-handed, was impossible.

Muttering to myself, I finished washing my hair and was trying to get the body wash on my loofah when I heard Christian say, "Need some help in there?"

Startled, I jumped and dropped the body wash. The shower has glass doors and even though they were somewhat fogged up, there was no doubt in my mind that he could still see me.

"What are you doing in here?" I exclaimed while trying to cover up.

"I'm here to help you." His low voice penetrated the glass screen.

"I don't need any help, so get out."

No answer. He was quiet, too quiet especially since I could still see his blurry image outside the doors proving he hadn't left like I wanted. Feeling completely exposed, I bent to get the body wash and quickly put some on my loofah, running it all over me so I could be done and he would have no reason to stay. With my back to the glass doors, I hadn't known the door had opened until a blast of cold air hit my skin. I squealed and turned, immediately crossing my arms over my chest, but everything else was on full display.

"Christian! Shut the door." My face burned with embarrassment when he let his eyes wander over my arms and face, eyes narrowing at the bruises covering my skin.

His eyes met mine in concern, and I immediately averted my gaze to stare at the side wall of the shower. Out of the corner of my eye, I saw him reach into the shower and put his finger under my chin, soaking his arm and part of his shirt while turning my face toward his.

"Honey, I've seen you naked. Why are you embarrassed?" he asked in a soothing voice.

I shrugged because I didn't know, but it felt different this way. I felt more vulnerable.

Christian sighed and ran his hand around the back of my neck. "Talk to me."

I couldn't talk to him. How could I explain that the few moments I'd had with him meant more to me than any amount of time I'd ever spent with anyone else? Or that the only way I could be strong enough to turn away from him was by avoiding him, and that having him near me only made me weak. And that my greatest fear was that when his conscience was cleared of guilt and he decided to move on, I'd be left alone.

By him.

Again.

He'd crushed me last time.

If I was to let him in now, he'd destroy me this time. I knew the only way to save me later was to send him away now.

"I don't want you here," I whispered.

He smiled sadly. "I know you don't, baby. But you need me here. So let me help you." He paused, moving his hand so both rested on my face, his thumbs stroking my cheekbone. "Let me take care of you."

Meeting his eyes, I saw nothing but concern and what seemed like sadness, so I nodded because, in all reality, I did need help, whether I liked it or not. And because when he looked at me like I was the only thing that mattered, I wanted to believe it.

"Are you done showering?" he asked softly.

For the most part, I was done, and the water had turned cool anyway. "Yeah."

With one last amazingly gentle stroke of my cheek, he reached around me and shut off the water. Then he wrapped the towel around me before using a second one to carefully dry my hair. He helped me dry the rest of my body, and I tried to pretend it wasn't Christian. That it wasn't the man I'd been thinking about and dreaming of for the past few months. His sweetness and gentleness would only make it harder for me when he left.

While I held my towel over my breasts like a shield, Christian bent down and began to slide my panties up my legs and over my hips, settling them in place. His fingers brushed along my skin the entire way, causing a shiver to run through me. I knew he felt it. Honestly, there was no way he couldn't. I closed my eyes slowly while he repeated the same with my pajama bottoms. When he was done, he stood and leaned in until we were close, so close that the heat from his skin warmed me. Starting with his hands on my shoulders, he ran them down until they rested on the top of my towel, staring into my eyes intensely. I nodded for him to remove it and my eyes fluttered closed. He slowly removed my towel after I dropped my hands and carefully put my arms, one at a time, in the sleeves of my shirt. I purposely chose one that buttoned down the front instead of trying to get it over my head. Opening my eyes, I met and held his as he buttoned my shirt. After finishing the last button, he ran his hands up and around until they rested on the back of my neck.

Leaning down until his forehead was resting on mine, he asked, "Do you have any idea how beautiful you are?"

"Yeah, right." Tears welled in my eyes. I wasn't feeling very beautiful. "Bruises and all."

He tightened his hands around me, and clenched his jaw before saying, "Those bruises are symbols of a fighter. Because you fought, you're here with me now and I promise, you'll never be alone again."

He pulled back when I didn't say more and took my hand to lead me into my bedroom. Putting the sling back on was much easier with help, as was getting into bed. I thanked him while I felt myself drifting, not remembering until I was snuggled under my blankets how tired I'd truly been.

I didn't know that Christian sat in a chair beside my bed, watching me sleep.

Just like he had in the hospital.

Chapter Twenty-three

Lucy

Three days.

Three days of sleeping, eating, oh and sleeping some more.

Waking in the morning still groggy, I decided I'd taken my last pain pill last night. My shoulder felt pretty good and without the pain pills maybe I could be a functioning adult again. I wanted to get back to work, needed to start physical therapy soon, and get Christian moved out.

I couldn't say he hadn't been helpful because he had. He made sure I'd had my medication, that I ate, and he'd been more than supportive. I'd been sleeping through most of it, which had been good because I hadn't had a chance to get too attached, but now he was going to have to go.

Thankfully, after the shower the first night, we had a routine where I would shower myself, but call him in to help me get dressed. Very platonic. We became very good at being, well, very good. He was even decent with Landon, who, from what I understood, had been to my place every day to check up on me. Actually, he'd been one of many, according to Christian, who grumpily told me that his family obviously didn't think he was capable since they hadn't left us alone yet.

After I told Christian my plan to stop taking the pain medication this morning, he left for the drugstore to pick up something else for pain. He came back an hour later with a bag full of every medication ever made over the counter for pain.

I'd gotten off the phone with the physical therapist and had a plan to start next week, when the doorbell rang. Before I even got up from the table in the kitchen, Christian was at the door.

"Hello, who are you?" a woman's voice asked.

Mom? I got up and went to the door just as my mom and dad walked through. Looking at them with wide eyes, I walked slowly toward the living room where they were now standing.

"Hey," I called out awkwardly. "What are you doing here?"

They turned quickly toward me, and I saw the shock in their faces when they saw me. Unfortunately, the bruises had become an interesting shade of yellow and brown and were not easy to cover.

"Oh, my," my mom muttered and put her hand to her throat.

My dad recovered a little faster and came to stand in front of me, putting his hands on my shoulders, careful of my arm still in the sling. "Honey, how are you feeling?"

"I'm doing better, Dad. Thanks."

"And you have a man living with you now. This is new," my mom commented.

That was my mom. Appearances were everything. Shaking my head, I looked over my dad's shoulder.

"No, Mom. Christian's a friend who's staying with me while the investigation is open. He's in security." I added.

She nodded but didn't look convinced.

"Mom, Dad, this is Christian Dimarco. He's Ben's brother." I waited while my dad shook his hand and Mom nodded at him.

"Have the police found this person yet?" Dad inquired.

"No," Christian replied. "The police hit a wall in their investigation, so we have our team of private investigators working on it."

"We do?" I questioned. "I mean, you do?" I corrected when he smirked at me. "I didn't know you guys were doing that already. Aren't you waiting for Brody's friend to get here?"

"Maybe we should sit down, and I can update you." Christian suggested.

We agreed and walked into my small living room to sit down. My parents sat together on the couch while I sat on the chair with Christian standing beside me.

"Brody's friend, Striker, is here already. He came as soon as we called and told him what happened," Christian said seriously.

"Why would he do that?" I questioned. "He doesn't even know me."

"He wasn't happy that there were no witnesses and no leads, so he finished up what he had to and came early. It was obvious within the first few days that Luke and the officers on the case had no direction to go in, so a P.I. was the next logical step."

"Has he found anything yet?"

"No. Nothing yet. It's like this guy just disappeared." He reached down and took my hand in his. I glanced at our joined hands and back up at him to see him shake his head. "We'll find him."

I nodded and looked back to my parents, feeling uncomfortable. "So...does anyone want a drink?"

"No, we can't stay," my mom replied quickly. "We wanted to check in on you before we headed home." She and my dad stood, obviously ready to leave.

"Well, thanks for stopping by," I said quietly as I stood too.

My dad stepped up first to give me a hug and whispered in my ear to call him later and we would talk more. He knew as well as I did that my mom wasn't going to be swayed to stay any longer, so he wouldn't even try. Sometimes as a kid I wished he would try, but as an adult, I gave up. My mom gave me a kiss on the cheek and another nod to Christian while Dad was shaking his hand and asking him to keep them informed. And then they were gone. Duties as parents fulfilled.

Shutting the door behind them, I took a deep breath before I turned around. Embarrassed for myself and my parents' obvious lack of concern, I turned and headed toward the kitchen. I felt him move behind me before he wound his arms around me and clasped his hands together over my stomach. He rested his chin on my shoulder and squeezed. I closed my eyes and swallowed back the tears that always followed one of those moments with my parents.

"I'm sorry you were here for that," I whispered.

He stiffened. "I'm not. I don't ever want you to feel like you're alone."

I pulled away and finished walking into the kitchen. "I like being alone, Christian."

"I don't believe that," he said. "No one likes to be alone."

I reached into the cabinet for a glass and filled it with water from the tap before answering. "You're wrong. Some people like it."

"No," he insisted. "Some people accept it, but nobody wants it."

"What do you know about being alone, Christian?" I sighed. "You come from an amazing family who spends time together. I didn't have that. I am so used to being by myself that sometimes being with people is overwhelming and I can't wait to be alone again."

What I didn't tell him was how much I hated that I'd allowed myself to feel that way. That up until the day Ben befriended me, I thought my life was supposed to be spent alone. And that the longer he stays, the harder it will be for me to go back to the way it was.

"I like my life." I continued.

"I don't believe you." He began to approach me as I backed up until my butt hit the counter and he was standing in front of me. He put his hands on the counter on either side of my hips and leaned down to look into my eyes.

I'd learned he liked to be close when he was serious about something.

Or when he was trying to make a point.

I just wished it wasn't so sexy. Everything he's done has been so intense. Every move. Every whisper. Every touch.

I bit down on my lip without thinking about it and watched as his eyes left mine and landed on my lips. I rolled my lips together before taking a deep breath and letting it out slowly. He took a few steps closer and slowly raised his eyes back to mine.

"Don't do that," he stated sharply.

"Do what?" I breathed.

He ignored my question. "It's taking everything in me not to lift you onto the counter, pull off your panties, and make you scream my name. If it wasn't for that fucking sling and the fact that I know you're still in pain, I would do it." He pushed even closer until he fitted his body perfectly to mine. "I know you want that too." He moved his hands from the counter to my hips and pulled me forward until I could feel his hardness pressing into my belly. My face got hot and I licked my lips again. "I know because I can feel it. Because when I'm near, your face flushes and your breath hitches." He leaned in and his breath fluttered across my lips. "And when you lick your lips like that, I feel it in my dick." I shook my head to deny it, but he stopped me when he said, "You're not alone in how you feel." He put his forehead to mine before I could respond, "I'm not leaving you alone. Do you hear me? I'm going to keep telling you that until you believe it. If this works out the way I want it to, I don't plan to ever leave, but I'm definitely not leaving before we find the prick who hurt you."

I shook my head or tried to as much as I could with him being so close before saying, "You can't stay here, Christian."

He pulled back enough to put his hands on either side of my face. "I'm not leaving you alone."

I breathed a sigh of relief when his cell phone rang right then. He pulled it out of his pocket and looked at the caller ID before shaking his head.

"I have to take this."

I nodded, relieved for the space that put between us. He was right. We couldn't be near each other without being surrounded by each other. I watched him tense while he listened to whoever was talking until I heard him say, "Are you fucking kidding me?" He turned then and looked at me accusingly while still listening. "Yeah, I'll talk to her and get the whole story." A pause and then, "I'll call you back."

He pulled the cell phone from his ear and ended the call before looking back up at me. He looked angry. No angry was too soft a word. He looked pissed. "Was this the first time you were assaulted?"

Chapter Twenty-four

Lucy

I didn't want to talk about this. I couldn't talk about *that*.

"What?" I stuttered.

He walked back into the kitchen from the small hallway where he had been standing. "I said, was this the first time you've been assaulted?"

Shaking my head, I said, "I—"

"Don't lie to me, Lucy," he stated sternly. "That was Striker. He's calling Ben next for more information, so I'm going to hear this story eventually, but I'd rather it came from you."

I walked around him and back into the living room, needing some space. Turning around, I put my hands on my hips. "I don't know what an incident in college has to do with what happened recently."

"An incident?" His eyes widened in disbelief. "Is that what you seriously call being fucking attacked?"

Pacing, I ran my hands through my hair. "I don't want to talk about this." I always felt like screaming when I simply thought about that night, let alone when I talked about it. That had nothing to do with now. It was a long time ago, and nothing ever came of it.

Turning, I faced Christian. "How do you even know I was assaulted? The charges were dropped."

"Because Striker brought a friend along to work with us who's a fucking tech wizard and he dug where he wasn't supposed to and found the original police report. So now you tell me what the hell happened and why you dropped the charges."

I stared at him incredulously. "I didn't drop the charges. His dad was a judge. I think you can figure out how he only ended up in a drug rehab program. And I'm almost certain he didn't have a drug problem."

Christian only stared at me and then dropped his head and rubbed the back of his neck. "Okay, just tell me what happened, and we can go from there."

"I still don't understand what that assault has to do with this one."

Christian took a deep breath. "Striker thinks it may have been the same person."

I shook my head. That couldn't be right. Could it?

"That can't be right. I haven't heard from him in well over a year and haven't seen him at all. We didn't even have history with each other. We literally met for the first time that night and besides the police station, I never saw him again."

"Listen, they don't know, but it's an angle worth exploring." He walked to me and put his hands on the sides of my face. "The assault on you seemed personal, not random. Luke had mentioned that in the hospital. That's why he asked the questions he did when he talked to you."

"I—"

"No." Christian interrupted. "No more stalling. I want to know what happened to you that night. I want to know what it has to do with Ben, and maybe it will explain why you two are so close. Because I still can't figure that out."

I nodded. He's right. I am stalling. I backed away from him, putting some space between us, needing the distance.

I took a breath and started. "I was somewhat of an introvert in college." I huffed out a half laugh. "Actually, all through school. I was shy, especially with boys. I never really found where I fit, you know?" I looked up at him, and he nodded his understanding. "Anyway, I spent most of my college years studying and tutoring, not socializing. Until I met your brother." I paused and smiled, remembering that day. "He was so much fun. Within a few months, he had convinced me to go out more, always going with me. It was almost like I tutored him in English Lit., and he tutored me in well, life, I guess. We went to see bands, we danced. He even introduced me to his friends and their girlfriends. They were all nice. I was finally finding my place." I paused, looking down for a moment to gather my thoughts. "Because of all of that, I also found some confidence. So when Ben wanted me to go with him and his group of friends to a party the football team was having, I agreed."

"So you're telling me that you spent all that time together and were never more than friends?" He interrupted me.

I guess I didn't realize how much that was bothering him. I shook my head. "No. It was always more of a brother-sister kind of relationship. We never saw each other that way." I laughed. "Not to mention, he was already sleeping with half of the female student body or at least those were the rumors."

Christian grinned. "Yeah, I'll bet he was," he said. "Okay, so you went to the party…"

"Umm, yeah, we went to the party. It was okay, but I knew right away it wasn't my thing. I felt out of place with most of the girls there, but Ben was interested in someone, so I hung around. I also knew if I left, he would've left too, and he'd done that too often for me. It was my turn to wait for him. Most people seemed drunk already by the time we got there. A lot of sex was going on and not all behind closed doors." I blushed a little at that memory. That was definitely something I hadn't encountered before. "Anyway, while I was trying to morph myself into the wall by the door"—I chuckled at the memory—"a guy approached me. He seemed nice. I hadn't met him before, so I knew he wasn't a friend of Ben's, but he asked about him, so I assumed they at least knew each other. He wanted to know if we were together, and I explained we weren't. He handed me a drink he was holding, and that's when I noticed he had two cups with him. We talked for a while. He was funny and seemed really sweet. I felt dizzy at one point and assumed it was the beer because I wasn't much of a drinker, but especially wasn't a beer drinker. I always ordered the girly drinks when we went out."

"I'll bet Ben loved ordering those for you," Christian said sarcastically.

I laughed. "Yeah, he was always trying to turn me into a beer drinker." When I paused, Christian gestured for me to continue.

"So, I told Aaron, oh, that's his name. I think I left that part out. Anyway, I told him I didn't feel well, and he offered me his room to lie down. I'm pretty sure this is like every after school special ever written, but I felt weird and thought if I didn't lie down, I would fall down. I looked around for Ben but didn't see him and honestly didn't try too hard to find him. I followed Aaron to his room and sat down. He got me a glass of water from the bathroom, and while he was in there, I sent Ben a text, but it didn't make much sense." I stopped, not sure I wanted to continue. I closed my eyes for a second and when I opened them, Christian was standing in front of me. He took my hand and led me to the couch. He sat first and then pulled me down sideways to sit across his lap. He didn't let go of my hand.

I swallowed hard. "Now I only remember parts. I always assumed that was why the police couldn't make the charges stick. Well, that and the fact his dad's a judge. I remember him kissing me, and I remember trying to leave, but he got really physical. I ended up back on the bed somehow, and he…" I paused, shaking my head. "I'm sorry Christian, I only remember bits and pieces from there."

"Did he rape you?" he growled.

Tears hit my eyes, and I tried to swallow them back, but I wasn't so lucky this time. When one roll down my cheek, I lifted my hand to brush it away.

"He tried. Ben got to me in time. You know, before he could finish. He had used his hands and fingers up to that point."

He let go of my hand and wrapped his arms around me, holding me tight. I didn't realize how much I needed that until the moment his arms tightened. I snuggled in closer, feeling his warmth surround me like a blanket. "What happened when Ben got there?"

I shrugged. "I don't remember. I heard a lot of yelling, but rumor was he pulled him off me and threw him against the wall. I guess he covered me up then and carried me out. We went outside, and he called the police. At least that's what he said. I was passed out by then."

He pulled me close, and I laid my head on his chest just below his chin. He squeezed me again before saying, "Remind me to thank Ben. Then what happened?"

"The next day when I was coherent again, Ben dragged me to the police station, and I gave my statement. Ben had already given his the night before. I found out they were holding Aaron until they interviewed me and all the witnesses. Of course, no witnesses came forward, so it was only Ben and me. They had done tests at the hospital and found that I was, in fact, drugged, but because no one saw Aaron do it, they couldn't use that. Honestly, it was a mess. Everything I said, he denied, and it became a he said, she said. The only good thing was that they had drug tested him as well because they found drugs in the house, and found that he had taken something. I never asked what. I didn't care. In the end, that's all they had and because he was a first-time offender, they let him go with the option to complete an inpatient rehab program. I haven't seen him since."

"So that's why Ben is so protective of you," he surmised.

I nodded and felt his chin rub the top of my head. "He feels guilty, and he shouldn't. He says if he hadn't talked me into going to a party I wouldn't have normally gone to, then none of that would have happened. So after all of that, we became really close. I think he completely took on the role of big brother then."

"So why did he bring you home with the pretense of being your boyfriend?"

I startled when my phone started ringing and pulled it from my pocket.

Ben.

I sat up completely. "Hey."

"Jesus, Lucy. I just talked to Striker. Did they tell you they think it could be Aaron?" He sounded completely pissed.

"Yeah, I'm here with Christian now, and that's what he said."

"Did you tell him what happened?" he asked quietly.

"Yeah. Well, as much as I remember."

There was a short pause. "Put me on speaker."

I pulled the phone from my ear and pushed the speaker button. "You still there?"

He ignored me. "Chris."

"Yeah, brother, right here."

"Are you guys honestly thinking it could be him?"

"Well, with the story Lucy told me, it's definitely possible, but I'm not sure what his motivation would be now."

"Revenge," Ben responded immediately.

Christian sat up straighter and took the phone from my hands. I could see the frown on his face when he spoke. "Revenge for what? The rehab stint?"

"No. Well, probably some of that, but he also lost his place on the football team and he was a senior headed to the draft," he stated.

"What?" Christian exclaimed.

"Yep. He was cut as soon as there was a hint of the assault charges, but the drug charges cemented it. They have an absolutely no-tolerance policy." Ben paused. "I think I heard he tried to use his father's pull to get him a spot on a team after rehab, but there were no bites. That shit comes with bad publicity for any team, and I'm betting he wasn't valuable enough for a team to be bothered with that."

Christian smiled an evil smile. "Well, we definitely have a motive."

"Wait, why me? Why didn't he come after you, Ben? You pushed as hard as I did for those charges to stick. Don't you think if it was him this time he would want to hurt both of us?"

"No way. He's too much of a pussy to come after a man. He does this shit to women because he goes in with the upper hand in his size alone."

That made sense.

"Alright, I've gotta go. I have to finish up few things here, and then I'm coming home for a few days," Ben said.

"Ben–" I started.

"No, Luce. I already made up my mind. I'll see you later tonight."

"Ben…" Christian called out before he could hang up.

"Yeah?"

"Thanks, brother."

"For what?" Ben asked.

"For always protecting her," Christian said with so much sincerity in his voice that I felt tears in my eyes again. I knew that had to mean so much to Ben. I hoped those few words would lessen the weight of the guilt he'd been carrying around.

After a long pause, we heard, "Thanks, man," followed by a click, letting us know he disconnected.

I hit end on my phone and stood. "Now what?"

Christian stood, pulled me into his arms, and smiled. "Now we go see the boys."

Chapter Twenty-five

Lucy

"None of this makes sense to me," I said, feeling frustrated.

We'd had a long talk, the boys and I, about my history with Aaron. The boys, of course, being Brody, Jax, and now Striker too. They were already waiting for us when we got to their offices because Christian had called to tell them we needed to talk. When I was introduced to Striker, he was a little intimidating at first glance, but the more we talked, the more I became comfortable. At first, I thought his size bothered me because he was huge. I mean, I thought the Dimarco boys were big, but he made them look scrawny. He had to be two hundred and fifty pounds of pure muscle and at least six feet five, if I had to guess. But as I talked to him, I wondered if it was the look in his eyes that actually intimated me. Or maybe the lack of emotion in his eyes was a better description, as he wore such a vacant expression. I couldn't help but wonder what or who had put it there.

They had me retell my story, and the best word I could think of to describe it was uncomfortable. It was hard to read their reactions, but tense looks were flashing back and forth. Christian then filled them in on what Ben had told us, which was information Striker already had.

"What part?" Jax asked.

"Well, I guess I don't understand what beating me up in an alley would gain him."

After a lot of awkward looks, Brody finally spoke up. "Honey, we don't think his plan was only to assault you."

I shook my head, but then it was like the light bulb finally clicked on. "He wanted to finish what he started?" I whispered.

Brody nodded. "I think that's exactly what he wanted to do," he said quietly. "His form of punishment. Take something from you like he feels you did to him."

"There's more to this, though," Striker interjected. "He's been off the grid for about three months now." Striker stood and paced a little before turning back to the group. "Lucy, I know you said you didn't think he had a drug problem at the time of your assault, but he did two back-to-back stints in rehab. Both arranged by his dad, according to the paperwork."

"Isn't that information confidential?" I narrowed my eyes, "How did you even see the paperwork?"

He smirked. "Might be best if you don't have that information."

Okay. Must be the new tech wizard.

"What does that have to do with anything?" I asked.

"Well, in my opinion, if he's using drugs, we're not dealing with a logical person. We are not dealing with someone who is making rational decisions. Add that to his anger over his lack of a football career, and what we are dealing with is a time bomb."

"I agree." Jax nodded. "We need to find him, and we needed to do that yesterday."

"What about Luke? Can't we go to him with the new information?" I asked.

"Already did," Brody confirmed. "He can't act in any professional capacity because we have no real evidence that the dickhead was involved, but he was able to get me a list of some dealers and locations that the department knows of and watches. At least we have a place to start."

I was guessing the dickhead was Aaron. The boys kept talking and strategizing, obviously dismissing me, for which I was grateful.

I looked toward Christian, who had been quietly sitting beside me the entire time. He smiled at me before saying, "You did good, Luce. I'm proud of you, baby."

I tried to ignore the warmth spreading through me at his comment, but it was impossible. Just having him there made this easier, and honestly, I couldn't have imagined doing it without him. I realized I was staring at him and felt heat moving up my neck. God, why was I always embarrassing myself with him?

The room got quiet, and I looked back toward the table where everyone was once again sitting. I watched Jax look toward Brody, smirking. I narrowed my eyes. What the hell was so funny? Cocking my head to the side, I looked back and forth between the two of them until they noticed me and stopped smirking. Hearing Christian chuckle beside me, I shifted my eyes to him and glared.

He leaned into me, and whispered, "It's funny as hell, baby, that you're the only one here who doesn't get it."

"Get what? And stop calling me that," I hissed back in a whisper.

"Us." He motioned between us. "And no, I won't stop calling you that, *baby*."

"There is no us," I said adamantly, still trying to keep my voice low.

He started to answer, but I shushed him. He looked surprised, shocked actually, that I did that. "Did you shush me?"

I heard the barely contained choking of laughter from the table.

"I'm not doing this here." I nodded my head toward the table while still looking at him.

"I don't think I've been shushed since we were kids screwing off in church." He laughed and looked toward Jax and Brody. They nodded in agreement and of course joined in the laughter. Okay, I was done with this.

"So, what do I do now?" I questioned, interrupting the joke fest.

"What do you mean?" Jax asked.

"Well, I feel like I need to help somehow. You know, help find Aaron or lure him out or something."

"Lure him out?" Christian said incredulously. "Are you crazy?"

"No, I'm not crazy." I huffed.

"You have a fucking sling on your arm, and you want to lure out the bastard who made you need it?"

"It was only an idea." It hadn't been a great idea, now that I heard it out loud, but I wasn't about to admit that to him.

"This isn't a crime show, Luce. You don't just help out."

"You know, I wasn't talking to you, Christian. I don't need your input," I snapped, feeling a little humiliated.

I saw him lean forward and knew this was going to start a huge argument. Whatever he was going to say was bound to piss me off, so I braced.

"Lucy." Jax interrupted, and I turned to him, but not before sending one final glare Christian's way. "I understand you want to help, but you can't. Not with anything right now, anyway. We have a plan, and we'll stick to that for now. You need to focus on getting well and staying out of trouble."

He said that last part with a soft smile. I nodded and stood when everyone else did, relieved we were done. I started toward the door, feeling Christian close behind, saying something to Jax. I was done listening. I planned to do what Jax said and get back to my life.

At the door, I stopped and looked back at the room filled with a group of ridiculously hot men. I wondered how I ever got so lucky to be included in this amazing group of people, which made me think of Ben, who had started it all for me. He had taught me how to feel confident and speak up for myself. The only reason I was able to be involved in that room today was because of my friendship with him. Well, him and Christian, if I was being honest.

Minus the cop show comment I was still pissed about, he'd been nothing but supportive since the assault. I owed these men so much, and I was disappointed I had nothing but words to offer.

Realizing all eyes were once again on me, I smiled. "I can't tell all of you what you mean to me. What this means to me." I paused, choosing my words carefully. "I won't ever forget this. I won't ever be able to repay this. But I promise I will spend the rest of my life trying."

Chapter Twenty-six

Lucy

The ride home from the "meet with the boys" started out fairly quiet. I didn't have enough experience to know if Christian realized I was still mad, and that was making me crazy.

When I couldn't take it any longer, I blurted out, "I hope you know I'm still mad at you."

He huffed. "Yeah, well, I'm still mad at you."

Mad at me? "For what?"

"You're shitting me, right?" He glanced over at me.

"Umm, no," I replied. "Wait, do you mean for telling you I didn't need your opinion?"

"No. That sounded ridiculous." He waved his hand around. I gritted my teeth while he continued. "How could you even suggest putting yourself in danger again?"

"I only wanted to help."

Sounding impatient, he raised his voice. "They don't need your help, Lucy. This is what they do." He slapped his hand against his chest. "What I do when I'm not babysitting."

"Babysitting!" He cringed as soon as the words left his mouth, but it was too late.

"That's not what I meant." Sighing, he called, "Lucy…"

Thankfully, we were at my apartment already so I could get out of the car without it still moving. I was out before he could finish and walking as quickly as I could to the door.

"Lucy. Come on," he called.

"I don't need or want you here, Christian. I think I've been clear on that." I didn't look back but knew he was behind me because his voice had gotten closer. I got to my door first but realized I didn't have my keys. Damn it. I waited with my back to Christian as he approached, still standing in front of my door. I felt him get close behind me and reach around with the keys. He unlocked the door but held the knob so we couldn't go in.

"That wasn't what I meant," he growled. "You know that, Lucy."

He reached his other arm to circle around my waist and pull me back against him. I stiffened but refused to say anything. I heard him sigh before he released me and pushed the door open.

I saw his clothes sitting in my living room, and without thinking, I jumped into motion. I grabbed his duffel bag from the corner of the living room and started throwing clothes in it.

"What the hell are you doing, Lucy?" He seemed tired all of a sudden.

I almost felt bad for a minute, but then I remembered his patronizing comments and kept packing his stuff. I walked around him to go to the bathroom where I found all the toiletries he had in there. Realizing there was too much to carry with only one arm, I decided I would need to make two trips. I loaded up the first bunch and walked back into the living room to his bag. He was standing in the middle of the living room, rubbing the back of his neck and shaking his head. I threw the handful in the bag and turned to walk back to the bathroom when he grabbed my arm and spun me around, getting right in my face.

"I'm not leaving," he said calmly.

"Yes, you are." I replied just as calmly.

"I already told you I didn't mean what I said. It came out wrong."

"Did you mean to embarrass me in front of the guys today?"

"How did I embarrass you?" he inquired, genuinely confused.

"You treated me like an idiot with your cop show comment," I said, quietly, looking at the floor. I shouldn't have looked back up. Maybe if I hadn't, it wouldn't have escalated. But I did. And I watched him trying to contain an obvious smile.

"You're an ass!" I pulled my arm from his grasp.

I started to walk around him, but he blocked my path.

"Move," I demanded.

"Nope." At least he was no longer smiling. "You know you weren't so innocent either with your comments. If I remember correctly, you were giving as good as you got."

That was probably true, not that I would admit it. "Just move, Christian."

"Are you fucking shitting me with this?"

That was it. I was so frustrated! "No, I'm not shitting you with this. I want you to leave. I want to go back to my life, and I want you to go back to your life."

"What fucking life?" he roared, and I began moving backward. "The one where you're not in it? That's what you want? The one where I'm so fucking miserable that even I don't want to be around myself?" He kept hollering while he started walking toward me. "The one where I wake up in the middle of the night, in a fucking sweat because I was dreaming about you…" He was right in my face now and leaned down, saying, "…again?"

I don't know what happened, but I snapped. I reached my hand up and around the back of his neck and pulled his mouth to mine. The kiss was not sweet or gentle. It was mean and angry and amazing. He pushed his tongue into my mouth and grabbed my waist with his hands, pushing me until my back hit the wall. He jerked my hips until he was rubbing his hardness against me, and I was groaning. He stopped the kiss when neither of us could breathe but ran his teeth down my neck, nibbling along the way and then soothing them with his tongue. It wasn't enough, and when my body felt like it was going to explode, I pulled him back up to my mouth and attacked. He groaned long and loud when his hands worked their way under the hem of my shirt until they were against my skin.

"Yes." I moaned, breaking apart our mouths. "Please."

"Please what, baby?"

"Touch me. Please. God, just touch me." I whispered against his mouth.

The knock on the door couldn't have come at a worse time.

"Fuck. Not now." Christian groaned when he pulled back and looked down at me. "We're not done," he said seriously, and I wondered if he meant with what we'd been doing or at all. I had a feeling he meant both.

He swung the door open and sighed, shaking his head. Ben pushed through the door, and I watched as his eyes landed on the open duffel bag with stuff haphazardly thrown in it. He obviously hadn't seen me yet since I was basically behind the open door.

He looked back behind him at Christian, smirking. "What the fuck did you do?"

I snorted. Man, I loved my friend. Of course he would take my side without having even heard the story. The snort gave me away. Ben turned to me just then and dropped his bag. I pushed off the wall and walked over to give him a hug, the entire time feeling Christian's gaze burning into me. I didn't know that Ben was grinning behind my back while staring at Christian.

"How bad did he fuck up?"

"Ben." Christian growled.

Pulling away from Ben, I turned to look at Christian before shrugging at Ben. "Only the regular amount."

"You're too nice, Luce. Chris is an overachiever. Always has been. I'm sure when he screws up, he does it all the way." Ben was laughing and holding his stomach, obviously finding himself hilarious. I couldn't help but join in and watch as Christian grinned.

"So, tell me about the meet with our boys today." He looked back and forth between me and Christian.

"Christian can. I'm going to grab a drink. Do you guys want anything?"

They both shook their heads, so I headed to the kitchen and got a glass of water. I listened as Christian told the abbreviated version of today's meeting and decided I was starting to feel more pain, so I grabbed some ibuprofen from the bottle and then went to sit on the couch. There was another knock on the door, and Landon pushed through. I gave him a small wave as he joined the conversation with Ben and Christian. Leaning my head back, I realized how tired I was and closed my eyes.

I didn't know I'd fallen asleep until I woke up and the room was considerably darker.

"How are you feeling?" I looked over to the chair in the corner of the room and saw Landon watching me.

"Umm, okay, I guess. Wow, how long did I sleep?" I inquired.

"A few hours. Ben and Chris left a little while ago to meet with their brothers, so I decided to stay and hang out with you."

"Because I'm such great company?" I joked.

Landon laughed and stood. "Are you hungry? I got some takeout a little while ago. I thought you might like some."

"No, thanks. I'm good right now."

He nodded and sat back down, but beside me this time.

"I'm surprised Christian left." I grinned. "I don't think I've spent one minute without him these past few days."

"It took some convincing." Landon huffed. "So what's the story with you two anyway?"

I figured this conversation was coming, but I wasn't prepared. "I don't know. Sometimes I think he feels guilty."

"Guilty for what?"

"I don't know," I reiterated. "We weren't very nice to each other after we first met. Him more than me, of course." I laughed.

Landon grinned. "I don't think that would make him stay here like this."

"Doing it for Ben?" I said.

"Lucy, are you really this naïve?" He turned to face me fully. "I mean, you get this is more for him, right?"

I shook my head. I opened my mouth to respond, but he held up his hand.

"Just hear me out, okay?" I nodded. "I know what kind of guy he is. We aren't that different, actually. What I know is that if he didn't have feelings for you, there's no way in hell he would sleep here. On your couch. He would have set up somewhere to keep you safe or had someone else do it. He wouldn't leave you hanging, but he sure as hell wouldn't have made himself your roommate." He paused, and I waited, curious where he was going with this. "I only want you to be happy and safe."

"Landon, I appreciate this. I really do, but Christian and I are in a weird place, and I honestly don't think we've made any decision about what we are to each other. I know I feel safe with him here, but I also know I don't want any relationship that forms out of fear or duty or, even worse, guilt."

I was surprised Landon was talking about this with me. This wasn't something we ever did. Relationship talks. His or mine. Not that I'd ever had any relationships before. He still deserved my honesty.

"I like him," I admitted quietly. "But I'm not sure I want to. Or if it's even healthy for me." I turned back to Landon. "I do know that right now is not the time to make any big decisions."

"I get that, but just remember, if this isn't for you what it seems to be for him, then maybe you need to have that talk."

Nodding, I looked at Landon and realized he looked sad and reflective. It was hard to tell, but it was there, and it was something I'd never seen before with him. "Did that happen to you?"

I didn't think he would answer, but he turned back and leaned forward, putting his elbows on his knees. "You know the worst part, Luce? I never even saw it coming. I was the naïve one."

Laying my hand on his back, I rubbed slowly when tears stung my eyes. When did we become this? We'd always been close, but we'd never discussed our emotions.

"Don't be that girl, okay?"

It was obvious the conversation was over when he stood and walked to the kitchen. I watched him grab a beer from the refrigerator and drink what looked like half the bottle in one shot.

At that moment, I realized he had a whole life I knew nothing about. More importantly, I vowed I would never let distance come between us again. I wanted him to stay close so I could keep building the relationship with him that I never knew I needed.

I also realized at that moment that I might be *that girl,* and I promised myself to do something about it.

I just didn't know what that was yet.

Chapter Twenty-seven

Lucy

"No!" I screamed. My body was shaking, and I was sweating. Looking around, I was desperately trying to remember where I was when I realized I was in bed, having one hell of a nightmare. The door slammed against the wall, and I looked up to see Christian standing there, in the doorway, gun in hand. In only his black boxer briefs. That was a really good look for him. Was it normal to be completely turned on and scared out of my mind at the same time?

"Jesus, what happened?" He looked around. "Are you okay?"

"S-s-sorry," I stammered. "I think I had a nightmare."

I watched him visibly relax and lower his gun. I heard the safety click back in place while he was walking toward the bed. He then laid it on my nightstand and sat down on the side of the bed facing me.

"I was worried this might happen," he said quietly. "I think the pain meds kept you sleeping so deep and so relaxed the nightmares couldn't get to you, but now that you're not taking them, they're probably going to creep up on you."

He sounded so calm when I felt anything but that. I nodded but still felt my body trembling. He gently pushed my body into the middle of the bed and crawled in beside me.

"What are you doing?" I asked.

"Sleeping with you."

"I don't think that's a good idea," I argued.

He rolled to his side and propped up on his elbow. "I don't care what you think right now. I'm not going to be in another room while you're suffering through these nightmares alone in this one."

"Christian—" I started.

"And I'm not arguing with you about it either. So roll your ass over so we can get some sleep."

"Christian!" I snapped.

Before I had the chance to say more, he carefully rolled me to my side, slid his arm beneath my head and his other arm around my waist, careful to put my arm in the sling on top of his arm. He edged me back until I was tight up against him, and he buried his face into the side of my neck.

"How the fuck do you always smell so good?" he muttered.

Admitting defeat, I relaxed back into him because it was comfortable, and if I was being honest, I didn't want to be alone. I immediately felt his warmth surround me, and I breathed in his intoxicating scent. "I'm a girl. We always smell good," I said back in an equally low voice.

He snorted. "I know for a fact that isn't true. I know some girls who smell worse than guys do."

"What the hell kind of girls do you hang out with?" I giggled when I heard him chuckling behind me and realized he'd done the impossible. He made me forget that I was alone and afraid only a few minutes ago.

"Thank you," I whispered so low I wasn't sure he even heard me until I heard his deep voice say something beautiful.

"You never have to thank me, baby. Don't you know by now that I'd do anything for you?"

I did know that.

So began the pattern of him sleeping with me every night. We never talked about it. We just crawled into bed every night together, and he wrapped himself around me. I still had some nightmares, but they were never as bad as the first night, and he was there to tighten his arms and hold me closer.

It wasn't until the third night of this that I realized what I should have a while ago. I was falling in love with him.

I should have talked to him about us.

I should have listened to Landon.

What I shouldn't have done was exactly what I did.

I had no idea that one small decision would start a chain of events so terrifying.

I had no idea that one small decision would lead to the biggest regret of my life.

Chapter Twenty-eight

Lucy

"I'm going back to work," I announced.

"No, you're not." Christian replied without even looking up from his phone.

"Yes, I am, and I already talked to my boss, and she agreed it's fine to go back."

I watched as he set his phone on the counter beside his coffee cup and slowly lifted his head to look at me.

"She said it was okay?" he asked, sarcastically.

"Christian." I sighed. "I—"

"I didn't realize she was in security," he continued, still sarcastic.

"Don't be a jerk." I frowned.

Completely ignoring me, he continued, "I also didn't realize she was working this case with us."

"Stop it."

"It's not safe. You're not going back yet." He picked up his coffee and took a drink.

It was the morning after my realization, and I needed to put some distance between us. I needed space so I could think. So I called my boss, and she agreed to let me work from the office only and do as much as I could over the phone. She still had the others doing my home visits for now, but this would definitely help reduce some work for them.

"It is safe, Christian. Our building has a security guard, and I would only be working from the office." He looked up at me when I began talking again but was frowning.

"No." He shook his head.

Time for the big guns.

"I already talked to Jax, and he said it was fine," I blurted.

"You what?" he inquired quietly.

"I didn't think you could make a reasonable decision."

"So, you don't trust me? You don't trust me to do what's best for you?"

"No, I do. Of course I do. But it's been over a week, and I want to get on with my life. I can't just keep sitting around here."

"You aren't. You go to physical therapy."

"That's three times a week, Christian, and I already have those scheduled so I can leave work early and go."

Just when I thought he was about to concede, the doorbell rang. Oh well, I was going whether he liked it or not. He walked away to answer it, and I followed, curious who was here this early.

"Hey, man." Hearing his voice, I looked around Christian and smiled when I saw who was on the other side.

Jake.

I hadn't seen him in a while. I heard he had been in to visit, but I was always asleep.

I walked over to him and gave him a hug.

"How're you feeling?"

"Great." I smiled. "Hey, guess what? I'm going back to work today."

He looked at me and smiled before looking over at Christian. The look on his face told the story of his disapproval, and Jake raised his eyebrows before looking back at me.

"Is that right?"

I nodded, liking the idea of going back the more I talked about it. I was excited to get out of this apartment.

"So how's grumpy here taking it?" He gestured toward Christian with his thumb.

"I think you know the answer to that." I was positive I heard Christian growl.

He smirked while I grabbed his hand and led him to the couch to sit down. "How are you? How's Julie?"

"I'm okay." He shook his head. "And Julie's Julie times ten right now."

"That doesn't sound good," I said.

"Nah, it's fine. We're figuring it out."

He would have been convincing if he didn't look so sad, but I didn't say that. Instead, I nodded and smiled.

"So what are you doing here?" Christian asked.

"Checking on one of my favorite girls." He smiled.

"And…" Christian waved his hand, signaling him to continue.

I watched as Jake leaned forward and put his elbows on his knees. I heard him sigh and realized he needed his brother now.

"I'm gonna get dressed," I said as I stood.

Jake stood with me. "You don't have to go, Luce. I can talk about it with you here."

"No, that's okay. I'll give you guys some time. Besides, I need to get ready for work." I purposely looked at Christian when I said that, daring him to say something, but surprisingly, he didn't.

I took a shower and got ready for work in pretty good time for only having the use of one arm. I didn't even need to yell for Christian to help, so I was proud of myself. I took my time making the bed and cleaning up around the room because I was trying to give the guys time to talk, but after I ran out of things to do, I decided I had to go out. Walking out, I noticed Jake had already left, and Christian was on the phone.

I realized I was walking in during a conversation with Jax when I heard, "Yeah, well next time Kasey wants something you don't want for her, I'll be sure to call and offer my opinion." Then a pause before, "Fuck you, man. You know what this is, and you knew I wouldn't appreciate your fucking input."

I walked to Christian and stopped right in front of him while he finished. "Yeah, well, I hope for your sake you can keep that promise."

He ended the call, slid his phone in his pocket, and curved his hand around the back of my neck to pull me closer.

"You serious about this?" he asked. "You're okay with putting yourself and other people in danger?"

I closed my eyes and then opened them slowly, looking in his eyes. "I know you would never let anything happen to me or anyone else."

He nodded. "No, I wouldn't, but I can't protect you there like I can here."

"I understand. I really do, but we have no idea when this will end or if whoever this was will even come after me again. I can't pause my entire life indefinitely." I paused with a small smile. "Please. I need you to be okay with this."

Hoping he could understand my need to get back into my daily routine, I waited for his answer. It didn't take long.

"Yeah, I get it. I'll make it happen for you." I started to thank him, but he interrupted me by saying, "But you need to do everything we tell you to do. No arguments."

I nodded enthusiastically and smiled. "Whatever you say."

He grinned. "I'll always like that answer."

Chapter Twenty-nine

Lucy

"Did you get that new referral I put on your desk yesterday, Lucy?" I looked up from my desk to see Mrs. Hastings, or Marie as she keeps telling me to call her, walking toward my desk.

"Yes. I already made first contact. Molly said she can do the first home visit when it's needed." I smiled.

"Excellent." She continued by me to her office.

It had been eight days since I started back to work, and I was remembering why I love my job. It had to be the toughest and most gratifying career I could have ever chosen for myself. Marie had been amazing working around my needs and my limitations. I really couldn't have done home visits anyway with the sling on, but she was supportive enough to give the guys time to track down Aaron for questioning.

Christian did exactly what he said he would do and set up security for every possible situation. He wanted Luke to place a cop at our offices, but there wasn't enough manpower in their department to lose an officer all day, every day. He settled for having daily meetings with our security guard who, so far, hasn't seemed too annoyed by that. Artie was a retired cop himself, so I figured he was probably better trained than most, not to mention more patient.

There had been absolutely no break in the case.

Aaron was still in the wind. I was learning hot security guy talk, and I learned this meant they couldn't find him. Striker and the new tech guy, whose name was Kyle, had been researching Aaron and were even more convinced he'd had something to do with my attack. I hadn't met Kyle yet, but I was picturing Clark Kent glasses and superhero T-shirts. I couldn't wait to meet him.

With Jax and Christian's help, I'd learned to pay attention to my surroundings more than I ever had before. I'd also stayed well within the boundaries they set up so I wouldn't do anything to cause problems.

Christian insisted on taking me to work and picking me up, which I'd accepted.

For now.

"Hey Lucy." I was taking off my sling when I heard my name and looked up to see Sam coming toward my desk. I smiled.

"Hi, Sam."

Coming around my desk, he leaned back into it and spun my chair until I was facing him, making me giggle.

"Guess you want my attention, huh?" I teased.

He grinned and then turned serious. "Okay first, how are you feeling? And should you be taking off that sling?"

"Pretty good. My shoulder definitely feels better. I can take off the sling some during the day now. I have the desk to rest it on so it's all good." I smiled. "And I've almost stopped jumping at every little noise, so that's better." I tried to joke, but Sam wasn't amused.

He took hold of my hand solemnly. "I don't know if that will ever be funny."

"I know," I agreed quietly. "So, what was second?"

Letting go of my hand, he pushed off the desk and stood in front of it, facing me. "Right, second. Have you heard the news on the Mills' case?"

"No. What news?" I asked.

"Mr. Mills agreed to an inpatient drug rehab program." He smiled.

"He did?" I was shocked. I never thought he would agree to that. "That wasn't part of his probation, was it?"

He smirked and sat in the chair in front of my desk. "Nope. Just said it was time. Left Morgan with his sister and signed the papers we needed to conduct visits there now."

"Have you been there yet?"

"Yep. Nice woman. Nice neighborhood. She's single and only twenty-five, but she is a full-time RN, so she's capable of taking care of Morgan. I think it's going to be a great fit."

"How long is the program?" I asked.

"Six months. Apparently, he's been hiding a very significant drug problem. I talked to his sister, whose name, by the way, is Kara, and she said he wasn't like this until his wife, Morgan's mother, died two years ago. She's tried several times to get him help but was never able to convince him. She thinks the law and CPS being involved now might have been a wake-up call for him because his need for drugs was fueling his manipulations of the system."

"That's amazing," I said in disbelief. "I hope the treatment works for him. Morgan deserves her only remaining parent to be healthy."

Sam nodded. "I agree."

"I feel really bad right now, though." I frowned.

He looked surprised. "Why would you feel bad?"

"I actually gave his name to Luke after my assault because he always kind of gave me the creeps. Luke said he had an alibi for that morning, so they had to dismiss him as a suspect."

"Don't feel bad, Luce. You did what Luke asked of you. Besides, I think that may have helped give him the push he needed."

I shook my head. "What do you mean?"

"Kara told me he had been to see her after a few officers had visited him, realizing the path he was on made him suspicious to others. She also admitted he didn't recall a lot of your meetings, so I'm guessing he was on something during them. It's no wonder he made you uneasy."

I nodded. "That would explain why he stared at me almost like he was looking right through me."

"Probably was."

"But the last few times I was there, the house looked pretty good. How was he keeping it together so well?" I asked, puzzled.

"He wasn't." He frowned. "Morgan was. Kara said Morgan would make sure everything was good so her dad wouldn't get into any more trouble. According to Kara, they were very close before her mom died, and she was protecting him. That's impressive for a ten-year-old girl if you ask me."

"Oh god, that's so sad. I hate when the kids become the parents."

He sat up straight and knocked his fist on my desk a few times. "Me too, but hopefully that won't be the case here much longer."

"Sam," I called out, and he turned back to look at me. "Maybe something good did come out of my assault."

"Nothing good ever comes from an assault." He smiled softly.

The moment his words stopped, his body jerked forward, and the sound of gunfire echoed through the room. His once sad expression now one of confusion.

Chapter Thirty

Lucy

The room around me exploded into motion.

I was pushed off my chair and shoved under the desk before Sam's body even hit the floor. I looked up in time to see Artie, our security guard, shot in the chest and fall backward, hitting his head on the floor hard enough to hear it crack. I watched his gun fall from his hand and reached out quickly to grab it. I realized I was too slow when a large, black military-style boot stomped down on it. I slowly lifted my head and looked up from boots, to jean-clad legs and finally to a hooded sweatshirt, with the hood up, shadowing a face.

He dropped his hand holding the gun until it hung by his side and pulled off the hood.

"We meet again," he said in a low voice.

I finally believed Striker when I looked into the eyes of my past. He looked different. Long gone was the popular football player, the ladies' man, and in his place was a person I didn't recognize. He was still built well, maybe even bigger than he was before, but his eyes were cold and filled with hate. All that hate was directed at me.

"Aaron," I whispered.

"Get up," he ordered.

I didn't move. I could only stare.

He leaned forward and roared in my face. "Get up!"

I flinched and put my hands flat on the ground to push up to standing when something warm seeped beneath my fingers. Shaking my head, I lifted my hands and looked at my palms only to realize they were covered in blood. Looking over at Artie, I saw his shirt saturated in blood and the puddle forming beside him on the floor. I was shaking and crying silently when Aaron grabbed a handful of my hair and pulled me to stand in front of him. I cried out and put my hand to my head where he was pulling, only to quickly pull it away when my hand touched his. I tried to hold my arm up that was no longer supported by my sling.

"Are you going to kill me?" I asked, voice shaking.

His face broke into an evil, maniacal smile. "Yes. But not quickly."

"Why? Why are you doing this?"

He leaned down until his face was so close to mine I could feel his pungent breath fan across me. I tried to shrink away, but his hand still fisted my hair, and he pulled me right back.

"You ruined my life, bitch. Now I ruin yours. Let's go."

He let go of my hair, wrapped an arm around my waist, and turned me so I was in front of his body, my back to his chest, and we started walking toward the door. I remembered Christian telling me to never leave and go somewhere else in this situation. I needed to find a way to remain in the same place so I could be tracked. But as hard as I tried, I couldn't think of any way to stop him from moving.

We walked by Sam's body, and I looked down to see his back saturated in blood, but I couldn't tell where it was coming from. I couldn't even call for an ambulance. I had to stop him. Right before we hit the front door of the building, I decided to try something, anything. Because he was going to kill me anyway, so something was better than nothing.

I shuffled forward and then quickly raised my foot to kick back into his shin as hard as I could. Unfortunately, it wasn't that hard because of the way he was holding me, but it was enough to surprise him, and he loosened his hold. I pulled forward to break the hold completely, but he grabbed my waist and pulled me back again. He slammed the side of his gun against my temple, and I immediately felt dizzy.

"Don't fucking try that again," he said in a scary, low voice. "I won't be so nice next time."

Walking the rest of the way to the door, he stopped and looked between the blinds toward the street. Then he backed up and looked around, turning me toward the back of the building.

"Where are we going?" I asked.

"Shut the fuck up. All you need to know is that today you'll get everything you deserve. Finally. I've been patient and waited a long fucking time for this, and your boyfriend isn't fucking it up again."

He started pushing me toward the kitchen, and I realized we would be going out the back door into the alley. I'd been avoiding the alley ever since I came back because of the flashbacks I was afraid of. I walked as slowly as I could until his arm moved from my waist, crawled up my body and his hand curled around my neck.

"Keep doing this, and we'll stop right here so you can watch me shoot the next person who comes through that door. You already have two deaths on your hands. How many more do you want?"

He was right. Two people I cared for were lying in pools of their own blood because of my selfish need to come back to work.

To get some distance from Christian.

I walked forward when a feeling of submission came over me. My head was throbbing, and my eyesight was a little blurry, which I was assuming was from the hit earlier on my temple. I realized if I went with him that everyone else, who may have already been on their way, would stay safe. Maybe once we got where we're going, I'd be able to come up with an escape plan, but right now I had to let him lead us away from here.

He pushed me through the door to the alley first and carefully checked both ways. Seeing the alley was empty, he moved us quickly toward a black SUV parked a little way up from the door. Moving with him, I prayed my plan would continue to work.

When we got to the side of the car, he shoved me into it, leaning against my back.

"I'm going to tie your wrists together before we get in so don't get any ideas about running." He growled in my ear. "I will shoot you. It won't be as fun for me as what I had planned, but the result will still be the same."

He moved the gun from my head, and we shuffled around a little. I assumed he was putting his gun somewhere, but I still had no intention of moving. I would be patient. I would be smart.

He pulled both of my arms behind my back and grasped my wrists together. Burning pain radiated from my shoulder to my wrist, and I gasped just as he pulled tighter. Taking a deep breath, I tried to calm myself, but I couldn't control the shaking that encompassed my entire body.

He pushed his body flush up against my back when my wrists were secured. I felt the shape of his gun pressing into the side of my back and realized he had put it in the front of his jeans. Running his hands up my body to wrap one arm around my waist and the other around my throat, he leaned in until his breath floated across my ear.

"I have waited so long for this." Jerking my neck to the side, he ran his tongue from where my shoulder met my neck and back to my ear. My stomach roiled from nausea and my body shuddered.

While his attention was still on me, I felt the air in the alley change. I stiffened. He probably assumed it was because of what he'd done, but it was something else. Then I heard the slightest noise that could have been anything moving around. An animal or even a leaf, but I knew better. He stiffened this time and lifted his head, pushing me back into the side of the car.

This was it.

He leaned back enough to pull his gun from his jeans, and I reacted. I pushed my ass out to get him off balance and kicked my foot back, praying I hit him anywhere. I only needed him distracted enough to run. I had no idea what I hit, but it pushed him back enough that I could drop down and push out of his hold. Without the use of my hands, I lost my balance and hit my knees but turned my head to see where he was.

I saw a flash of color pass by me before I heard a body hit the ground. Then I heard running and shouting, but as hard as I tried to turn, I was having trouble twisting my body around without my hands to help. Out of my right eye, I saw Brody come running toward me, and my emotions finally took over. I stopped struggling. Leaning my forehead against the door of the SUV, I started crying, shaking uncontrollably.

"I've got you," Brody said, placing his hand on my back. I felt a tug on my wrists as he cut the ties. "Can you walk?"

"Yeah," I whispered. With his hand on my arm, he pulled me up, and I turned toward the alley.

What I saw will stay with me forever.

Aaron was lying on the ground, and Christian was on his knees over him with his hands around his throat, choking him. Aaron's face was bloody and swelling, one eye already shut. Brody tugged on my arm to move me, but I couldn't. He was going to kill him while the others watched. Striker, Jax, Brody were all just standing there.

"Stop!" I screamed. Brody pulled me into him with his arm around my waist. My back to his chest.

"Jax, stop him! Why isn't anyone stopping him?" I struggled against Brody's hold.

"We will," Brody whispered in my ear. "He needs this."

What the hell was he talking about? Aren't they worried what would happen if he killed him? I heard the wail of sirens getting closer and closer. I kept struggling against Brody, but he wouldn't release me.

"Christian, stop it." I yelled, my voice breaking on a sob. "Please, stop it," I begged, crying so hard my body was shaking.

I watched his head swing toward me, and his eyes narrow when he caught sight of my face. He dropped his hold on Aaron immediately and stood, looking down at him with disgust. Brody turned me so I was against his chest now, crying and holding his shirt, soaking it with my tears.

"Brother, she needs you." I thought I heard him say, but there was so much commotion and the sound of boots hitting the pavement echoed in the alleyway that I couldn't be sure.

Brody's chest rumbled, and I assumed he was talking, but I couldn't hear him.

"Lucy?" Looking up, I stared into Luke's concerned eyes. "Can you answer some questions for me?"

I nodded my head and backed away from Brody. "I'm going to help the others if you're okay." He looked at me expectantly, and I nodded my head. He smiled sadly and walked toward Jax, who was talking to an officer. I took a minute to look around and noticed all the cop cars and police, along with a lot of EMTs.

I gasped and looked at Luke. "Inside. Artie and Sam," I said in a shaky voice. "Luke, you have to send someone inside. They need help."

He held my shoulders lightly and leaned down a little. "They're already being taken care of."

I nodded and released the breath I didn't know I was holding. "Are they okay?"

"I'll get an update on them as soon as anyone has any concrete information, okay?" he promised softly.

"Okay." I looked down at Aaron's body surrounded by EMTs.

"Lucy." I redirected my eyes to Luke. Lifting my hand to my temple, I squinted my eyes, trying to focus on him.

"What happened to the side of your head?" He carefully turned my head so he could look at it.

"He hit me." I closed my eyes when my stomach roiled.

"Hey, Jax!" he called out. "Get me an EMT."

"Lucy." I blinked my eyes open slowly when I heard my name. "Sweetheart, talk to me."

"What?" I whispered, shaking my head. It was almost as if I was in a bubble and everything around me was muffled.

An EMT approached, and Luke turned me over to him but promised to stay with me.

"Where the fuck is Christian?" I heard being yelled before a calming darkness overcame me.

Chapter Thirty-one

Lucy

Opening my eyes in the hospital felt like Deja vu. From the beeping sound of the machines to the smell that could only be described as the scent of sickness and fear, I knew exactly where I was. I also knew I wasn't alone. A sharp pain radiated across my temple when I turned my head to the side slowly and saw Ben and Landon talking quietly in the corner of the room.

"Hey," I whispered.

I watched as both of their heads jerked toward me, and Landon came rushing over.

"Jesus, Lucy, are you okay?" he asked with concern etched all over his face.

I gave a small smile. "I think so."

I watched Ben approach me, waiting for the smile he's famous for, but it never came.

"What's wrong?"

"Nothing Luce. Just worried about you," he answered.

"Don't lie to me, Ben." I narrowed my eyes. "What happened?"

He shook his head and glanced toward Landon, communicating without words. "I'm going to get the nurse." He turned and left the room.

"Landon?"

"It's nothing, Lucy. This whole situation has everyone upset," he admitted.

Both Landon and I looked at the opening door when we heard, "Hey, look who's up," being called from the doorway.

I smiled at the nurse who came in and began checking the machines and taking my vitals. I watched Landon and Ben make their way back to the corner and wondered where Christian was, and if he was all right.

"So, you've had a mild concussion, which could be causing some confusion. Can you tell me your name, birthdate, and who those two handsome men are?" the nurse inquired.

I gave her the information, and she said everything looked good, but she was going to page the doctor and have him check me out.

After the door shut behind her, I asked, "What happened with Aaron?"

"He's in the hospital but has guards on his door. He'll be released into police custody when he's physically able," Landon answered.

"When do they think that will be?" I inquired.

Landon shook his head. "No one knows, Luce. He has some recovering to do."

I looked at Ben, who hadn't spoken much. "Is Christian okay?"

With his hands on his hips, he dropped his eyes to the floor, shaking his head. "Fuck."

"What?" When no one responded and neither man would look at me, I impatiently repeated, "Ben. What?"

He looked at me with an angry expression. "How can you even ask about him?"

"What?" I whispered. "I don't understand. Did something happen?"

I could only wonder if he was in jail for protecting me.

Ben threw out his arms to the side, "Yeah, something

happened, Luce. Do you see him here? Do you see him here where he should be?"

"I…" I stammered with tears in my eyes.

"He should be here with you right now, taking care of you. But you know where he is? In his office. Drinking himself into a fucking stupor because he can't handle what happened to you. What he didn't protect you from again." He had slowly been raising his voice with every sentence until Landon put his hand on Ben's shoulder to calm him down.

A tear rolled down my cheek, and I lifted my hand quickly to wipe it away.

"Luce, I'm sorry." Ben walked toward me. He took my hand and sat down in the chair beside my bed. "I shouldn't be yelling at you. I'm just so pissed off right now, that's all."

I heard the door creak open and raised my eyes to see Jack and Anna walk through.

"What's with all the yelling?" Jack asked gruffly and looked at Ben. "You trying to get us kicked out?"

Anna rushed to the side of my bed, leaned down to kiss my forehead, and pushed Ben out of the way. Waving her hand at Ben, she forced him to move from the chair so she could sit.

Jack came over next to the other side of my bed and took my hand, leaning in to kiss my cheek.

"How are you feeling, darlin'?"

"Okay." I smiled softly.

"These two idiots bothering you? I can get rid of them if you want me to." He grinned.

I looked at two of my favorite people in the world and giggled at the affronted looks on their faces.

"Never." Jack chuckled and squeezed my hand. "Besides, I tried years ago to get rid of them, and it's impossible."

The door opened to the doctor next who went over my chart, asked me a few questions, and said I was free to leave when the paperwork was ready. I asked how long I'd been there, and he said

I'd completed the twenty-four-hour stay he required. This surprised me because I didn't think I had been there for more than a few hours, but I was definitely ready to go. I asked Anna if she would stay and help me for a bit, so she shooed everyone else out the door.

"You want to tell me why you wanted me to stay?"

"Is Christian okay?" I blurted out. She looked surprised, so I continued. "Ben said he wasn't doing great, and I'm worried about him."

Her face softened, and she took my hand again. "No, honey. He's not doing well right now, and he's certainly not handling this situation well at all." She frowned and shook her head. "Do you know what I prayed for when I was pregnant with each one of my boys?"

"Patience?" I guessed.

"Well yes, but I prayed for me to have that." She laughed. "I wanted my boys to have the same need to protect the ones they love that their father does. It's one of the things I love the most about Jack." She smiled. "My boys got that in spades, so I'm thinking I may have prayed too hard." I nodded in agreement and grinned. "Knowing Christian the way I do, I'd say right now he's having a hard time coming to terms with not being able to protect you."

"But…"

I started to speak, but she shook her head and patted my hand. "Give him some time. He'll figure it out. His brothers won't let him be until he does." She snorted. "Heck, what am I saying? His father won't let him be until he does."

"It wasn't his fault," I whispered.

"Of course it wasn't, honey, it was Aaron's." I nodded because as true as that was, he wasn't the only one to blame. I needed to accept my part in all of this. I just hoped I could live with the guilt.

I finished dressing a few minutes before Luke came in. I'd sent Anna away and told her I was fine, but the truth was, I needed some time to myself. She kissed my cheek and hugged me, saying they would see me soon, but that wouldn't be the case.

"How are Artie and Sam?" I inquired as soon as he walked through the door. I was ashamed I hadn't asked already, but seeing Luke sparked my memory.

He came over and sat in the chair facing the bed right across from my seat on the bed.

"They were lucky," he said. "Marie Hastings was in her office when she heard the shots and promptly called the police and then us, exactly like we'd gone over with her. I'm sure that went a long way in saving their lives."

"Not only their lives," I agreed softly. "How bad were they hurt?"

"Sam was shot in the back," he said, and I watched his jaw clench. "No one should ever be shot in the back." He ran his hand through his hair. "No vital organs were hit, but he had to have surgery to remove the bullet, so he has some recovery ahead of him."

I let out a long breath and smiled. "So he's going to be okay?"

"Yes. Looks good for him."

The way he said it made me think Artie's news wasn't as good.

"Artie?" I asked in a small voice.

He frowned. "Lucy..."

"Tell me, Luke," I insisted.

He nodded. "Artie was shot in the chest. The bullet missed his heart but lodged in his lung, and he had to have surgery to remove it."

Okay, that didn't sound too bad so far, so why did Luke look afraid to tell me?

"And...?" I prompted.

He sighed. "After the surgery, while he was in recovery, he suffered a stroke." He reached for my hand, but I pulled back and covered my face.

I wiped away my tears. "How bad was it?"

"We don't know yet. He's sedated right now, so we won't know what the long-term repercussions are for a while."

"Okay," I said softly. "Can I visit them?"

"Yeah, I can take you to see them." We stood together, and he took my hand. "They're alive, Lucy. That's what matters."

I picked up my belongings and walked to the door. Stopping before I opened the door, I turned to look at Luke behind me.

"That's not all that matters." I pulled open the door to walk out.

"Lucy…" he said, but I didn't turn. Instead, I waited for him to catch up and walk beside me.

"What about Aaron?" I asked.

He sighed. "He's here for evaluation and will be for a few more days at least."

"And then?" I encouraged him to continue.

"Well," Luke said, "he's facing a lot of charges, but the main ones are felony assault and attempted murder."

"Do you think his dad can get him off again?"

"Not this time, Luce. You're safe now," he stated.

But I didn't feel safe. Not yet.

"This is Sam's room," Luke gestured toward the door of a room a few floors down from mine.

"I'd like to go in alone."

He nodded. "I'll wait here."

Before pushing open the door to Sam's room, I turned back to see Luke already pulling out his phone.

I walked into his room and turned to the bed to see a woman sitting beside the bed, holding his hand, but his eyes were closed.

"Can I help you?" she asked.

"I was hoping he might be awake."

"Lucy." I jerked my eyes back to the bed to see Sam smiling at me.

"You're Lucy?"

I looked back to the woman at the same time Sam did.

"Denise, can you give us a minute?" he asked.

"Give you a minute?" She narrowed her eyes. "She's the reason you're in here. What could you possibly have to talk about?"

It was as if I'd been kicked in the stomach when she said aloud what I'd been feeling.

"Denise," Sam said sternly. "This was not Lucy's fault. Now, please go wait in the hall."

She got up slowly and walked by me without giving me a second look. After she was gone, I walked over to Sam and sat in the chair beside his bed. He leaned down and grabbed my hand.

"Hey, this is not your fault. I mean that."

And he did. It was a shame I didn't feel the same.

"How are you?" I asked.

"Pretty damn good, considering what it could have been."

He smiled, but I wasn't ready to joke about it. He squeezed my hand. "Lucy, look at me."

"I am," I insisted.

"No, you're not. If you were, you would see that I'm fine. That Artie's fine." That made me flinch. "We're alive. That's all that matters. Okay?"

I nodded and forced a fake smile. I was sure he knew it was fake, but he didn't comment.

"So, who's your friend?" I asked, desperate to change the subject.

"Ah, friend is too strong a word," he said. "That's my ex-wife."

"Oh." My eyebrows drew together. "That's strange."

"Yeah, it is strange." He smirked.

Shoot. I guess I'd said that out loud.

"I'm not sure what she's doing here. She came about twenty minutes before you, and I tried to pretend I fell asleep." He chuckled.

That made me smile.

"Hey, I got a real smile this time." He smiled.

I shook my head but couldn't help grinning. "So, when can you leave?"

"Couple of days. As long as everything continues to go well. But I'm not in any hurry."

That took me by surprise. Sam wasn't known for being still all that much. "Why?"

He smirked. "I have a night nurse I'm hoping will agree to give me a sponge bath."

This time, I laughed out loud. "You're a pig."

"No, I just try to make the best of every situation." He chuckled.

"Well, in that case, you may want to get rid of the ex."

"Yeah, I know," he grumbled. "I guess I'm going to have to man up and ask her what she wants. Because believe me, she always wants something."

"I didn't even know you had an ex," I admitted.

"I know. It's not something I brag about, trust me."

I looked at the clock on the wall and frowned. "I think I should get going. Luke's waiting for me in the hall, and I wanted to go see Artie before visiting hours are over."

"Thanks for coming, Lucy," he said sincerely. "I'll see you at work next week, right?"

I shook my head. "I don't think they're going to send you back so soon."

Standing up, I leaned over and gave him a hug. "Get better, okay?"

"I'll call you. You can keep me company while I recover." I nodded and walked to the door.

"Lucy," he called.

I stopped and looked back at him curiously.

"It's not your fault."

I nodded again, took a deep breath, and pulled open the door.

Walking into the hallway made me smile because I saw both Luke and Denise glaring at me. She pushed by me, making sure she hit my shoulder before going back into Sam's room.

"What the hell was that?" Luke asked, sounding frustrated.

"I think that woman needs to be on the mental health floor."

"Was it really that bad?" I inquired, still smiling.

He walked over, slung his arm gently around my shoulders, still avoiding the injured one, and we walked toward the elevators. Thankfully, the X-rays hadn't shown any additional damage to my shoulder, but it still hadn't healed completely from the surgery, so I needed to be careful.

"She's a nightmare. He's going to have a hard time scraping her off."

"They're already divorced," I said.

He looked at me with wide eyes. "Jesus, they're divorced? She's crazier than I thought."

"So how did you get the job of picking me up?" I asked.

"I was already here getting statements," he answered, "so I told the boys I'd get you. They're going to meet you at your place."

I nodded as we stopped in front of Artie's door.

"I won't be long."

"Take your time. I'll wait," he said.

I walked into Artie's room, expecting the worst. My eyes immediately went to the bed where I saw a pale, much weaker looking man than I had known at my office. He wasn't awake, so I looked at the chair beside the bed to see an older woman looking at me curiously.

"Hi." I gave her a small wave. "I'm Lucy." And then I held my breath, waiting for her reaction.

She stared for a moment before she nodded. Then she turned her head back to Artie again and was so quiet, I was sure I was being dismissed.

"How is he?" I inquired, needing to know something, anything before I left.

She turned her head back to me, but her expression was distant. "You know, I begged him to quit working." Her voice was so soft I had to strain a little to hear her.

I watched her eyes fill with tears before she turned her eyes from me back to Artie. "He was a police officer for thirty years and I was scared everyday he left for work until he came home. When he retired, I think I finally took a deep breath." She paused and shook her head, then wiped her eyes with a tissue. "Then he comes home one day and announces he's taking a security job. Says he doesn't know who he is if he's not protecting someone or something."

When the tears ran down my face, I made no effort to wipe them. "I'm so sorry."

She looked at me then with red eyes and nodded. "Me too."

I turned to walk away, knowing I wasn't welcome.

"Lucy," she called out.

I paused at the door, not wanting to turn for fear of what I'd see in her eyes. So I stayed there and dropped my head to look at the floor.

"Are you safe now?"

I took a deep breath and replied quietly, "Yes."

"Good. That's what he would've wanted," she said.

I wiped the tears from my face as best as I could before I left the room, but it was obvious to Luke the visit hadn't gone as well as Sam's had. He took my hand, and we didn't talk until we were in the car leaving the hospital parking lot.

"Would you mind dropping me at Mrs. Hasting's house? My boss," I clarified at his confused expression.

"I know who that is, Lucy, but I'm not sure that's a good idea. Don't you think you've had enough for today?"

"Please, Luke. I'll have her take me home after we talk." I looked over at him, pleading with my eyes and hoping he understood how important this was to me.

"Okay," he finally relented.

"Thank you. I'll text Landon and Ben when I'm leaving to go home."

He nodded but looked at me with an unhappy expression because we were both thinking the same thing. I hadn't mentioned Christian.

Actually, no one had mentioned him without me first bringing it up.

Pulling up to Marie's little house, I was happy to see her car in the driveway. I knew she wasn't expecting me, but after Luke had told me she was responsible for the police arriving so quickly, I felt like I needed to see her. She saved my life. I owed her so much more than a thank you.

I thanked Luke for the ride, knowing he would wait in the driveway until he saw me enter the house, and walked the few steps onto her porch. Hesitating before I knocked, I thought about Artie and remembered the sadness and fear I saw on his wife's face. For a minute, I felt like the guilt would consume me, and I pressed my hand against her door when my legs buckled. Knowing I didn't deserve her forgiveness, but praying for it regardless, I curled my hand into a fist and knocked quietly.

She opened the door to me, surprise evident on her face. Reaching out, she immediately pulled me close and wrapped me in a hug so tight that I couldn't contain the sob that broke free. Pulling me in and closing her door, she held me and we both cried for what felt like a long while. Her husband was kind enough to give us privacy, only coming into the room to check on us occasionally.

Marie sat me down next to her on the couch and explained what she had done while holding my hand. It was exactly what Luke had told me, and I thanked her over and over again until she told me to stop. I couldn't imagine the fear she felt at being in her office and hearing the gunshots without any idea who was on the receiving end of them. I told her I had seen both Sam and Artie, which she had also done, and knew Artie's health and recovery were both still questionable. She said she had also been in to see me, but I had been sleeping. We talked about work because she was missing two staff and a security guard for an indeterminate amount of time, but she told me to take as much time as I needed to recover and my job would be waiting for me. She had spoken with the two recent retirees from our office, and they had offered to come back and help out with cases until Sam and I were well enough to return.

After about an hour, I asked her to drive me home, claiming I was tired, and she happily agreed. She left to get her keys from the kitchen but returned with her husband, who said he would be the one to take me home instead. He offered me a smile, but we both knew he didn't trust her to be with me. She smiled apologetically and hugged me again before we left. I didn't blame him. How could I? He was protecting her, and I hadn't done that.

I didn't text Landon or Ben when I left Marie's house like I'd promised Luke.

I didn't text them when I got home.

I didn't text them when I packed my suitcase and wrote the note I'd planned on writing.

I didn't text them to tell them where I was going.

I just left.

And hoped they would do what I'd asked.

Chapter Thirty-two

Christian

The door to my office slammed open, and I blinked awake.

"Wake up, fucker!"

One of my brothers yelled. I would know those damn voices anywhere. I looked up from my desk and slowly raised my head.

"Get the hell out, Ben," I stated calmly.

Jesus, my head hurt. I looked over at the empty bottle of Jameson beside my arm and sighed. I didn't even remember finishing it.

I jerked back when a piece of paper hit my desk and an angry Landon was in my face. "Get the fuck up and find my sister."

What? I slowly blinked my eyes and looked past Landon to Ben. I watched Luke and Brody walk in and look at Ben.

"What's up, Ben?" Brody asked with a chin lift in his direction.

"Chris has something he wants to read to you."

I did? What the fuck was he talking about?

Landon grabbed the paper back, and I thought I heard him mumble, "Worthless." He handed the paper behind him to Brody. "You need to help me find her, man."

I stood while Brody read and watched the tic begin in his jaw.

"Shit," he mumbled. He looked at Luke, who was reading over his shoulder. "Call Jax."

Luke nodded and pulled out his cell, shaking his head.

Grabbing the paper from Brody's hands, I cringed when I looked down and saw the familiar handwriting.

I'm sorry. I don't know what else to say to anyone. I know you will all say that none of this was my fault, but we know a lot of it was. I need time to myself. I need time to deal with the guilt I feel, and I can't do it with all of you around me. Please understand. Please don't look for me. Just trust that I'm okay, and I'm doing what I need to.

Thank you so much for protecting me.

"What the fuck?" I swore. "What the hell happened? What happened to you staying with her, Landon?"

All eyes landed on me, and they were all pissed. Landon grabbed me by the front of the shirt and pushed me back until I hit the wall.

"Me? Where the hell have you been in all of this? You promised me you would protect her. I left her with you. My own sister, man, and now she's gone. So, I'll repeat, where the hell were you?"

I shoved him back. "I didn't protect her!" My skin was so hot it felt like my blood was on fire. "I can't get the fucking image of her on the ground out of my head! Hands tied behind her back." I started to pace. The anger consumed me. I wanted to go back to that alley and kill the bastard by slowly choking the life out of him. If Lucy hadn't called out, if I hadn't heard her voice, I don't think I would have stopped. I had to make them understand. Looking at the room full of men, but no one in particular, I called out. "I watched the EMTs put her in that ambulance." I grabbed the sides of my head to stop the vision from playing on repeat in my mind. "Knowing it was my fault because I didn't do my fucking job! What could you possibly want from me now?"

"I want you to find my goddamn sister!" Landon yelled right back at me.

"I can't protect her, man," I admitted in defeat.

"You can't standing here," he pointed out sarcastically.

"None of us protected her the way we should have," Brody said. "We thought we had her covered, and we didn't. But that isn't the point." He paused and looked back at Luke, who nodded. "The point is, we need to find her and bring her home."

"And this is about you, Chris," Ben said. "You either want her or you don't. If you don't, then tell us now. But if you do"—he leaned in toward me—"then get the fuck over yourself and find her."

I stared at both of them, my own guilt pounding in my head. Hearing them and knowing it was never a matter of wanting her. I'd always want her. But if we didn't find her soon, the chances of having her were nonexistent. I couldn't even imagine the hell she was living in. She was all alone with her guilt, pain, and fear.

Meeting Luke's eyes, and seeing the ever-present support there, I nodded. "Where do we start? I can't even fucking think."

"Go take a shower and wake the fuck up. We'll make some coffee, and by then, Jax and the others will be here," Brody said.

"Can you do anything legally to bring her back?" Ben stared directly at Luke.

He shook his head. "Not really. I have a partial statement from her, so I guess technically I could bring her in to complete that. But with everyone else's statements already done, I don't exactly need Lucy's to hold Aaron."

"But you'll need it eventually, right?" I asked.

"Eventually I will, yeah," Luke admitted.

I left my office and walked to the bathroom to take a shower, thanking Jax the whole time for putting a shower in when he had Jake do the remodel on the building. Its original purpose had been for the guys doing overnight surveillance or for a quick cleanup between jobs, but we all found ourselves using it more than we had anticipated.

I hurried through a cold shower, hoping it would wake me up, slowing only long enough to let the water run over my head and down my neck and back. Pressing my hands against the shower wall and picturing Lucy, I thought about the past few months and knew I would do anything to bring her back to me. Finishing up with a newfound confidence, I threw on a pair of jeans and a long-sleeved gray T-shirt before heading back out to the main room. I heard the sound of voices and realized they had moved to the conference room. Walking in, I saw almost the whole team was there. I got a chin lift from Striker and a distracted wave from Kyle, whose nose was already buried in a computer. I grabbed a seat and waited but not for long.

"What the hell's going on?" Jax asked from the doorway.

I looked at Ben and then over at the rest of my brothers, including Lucy's. "We need to find Lucy."

Luke handed him the note he was still holding.

"Fuck," Jax muttered. "I was afraid of something like this."

"So was I," Luke agreed.

"Why?" Landon asked.

Luke frowned. "She wasn't herself. She insisted on going to see Sam, Artie, and her boss last night. I didn't go in with her because I thought she needed that privacy, but I have no idea what was said to her." He looked over at Landon. "I assumed you or Ben would already be at her place when she got home." He shook his head and rubbed the back of his neck. "That's on me. I shouldn't have assumed."

"We should've been," Landon said, "but Lucy's always needed time to herself to process shit. I was trying to give her that." He looked over at Ben.

Ben nodded. "We talked about it and agreed she needed some space. It's who she is." He looked back at Luke. "That's on us, man."

"Alright, enough of the blame shit," Striker said irritably from the end of the table. "It doesn't matter who fucked up. We need some information if Kyle's going to have any luck tracking her."

He looked at Landon. "If you can give us the easy stuff, we can save a lot of time."

"Like what?" Landon asked.

"Personal shit. Birthday, banking info, friends or family she could be crashing with."

Landon nodded and moved to sit next to Kyle.

"She already turned off her phone." Kyle smirked at Striker. "I love a fucking challenge."

I looked around the table to see everyone grinning. We were going to find her. And then I was going to bring her home.

This time, I wasn't letting her go.

Chapter Thirty-three

Lucy

There was an advantage to having parents who preferred traveling more than spending time at home because when you needed to be alone, they had homes in different places you could use. Or at least mine did. A few I didn't think Landon even knew about, especially since he spent less time with our parents in the past five years than I had. I even had keys to them. Two of them were within driving distance. At least within driving distance for my car, so I figured I would try out both.

I was smart enough to know it was only a matter of time before they found me, especially if they put Striker on the job, but I still decided to leave. I'd taken out some cash from my account before I left the state for gas and groceries, knowing I wouldn't need much more. I had also turned off my phone. I wasn't hiding exactly, but I hadn't had any time to myself since I moved to New Hope, and I needed the space to think.

I'd made it almost two months on my own, and I knew time was about up. I needed to go home. I needed to tell Landon and Ben that I had come to a decision and was going to move on. I was leaving New Hope. It was time to start fresh and not be face-to-face each day with every bad choice I had made.

Especially Christian.

He left me. I got used to him being there, and then he wasn't. I wasn't even disappointed in him for leaving me in the end. I understood. I hadn't expected much anyway. But my feelings for him were strong, and I couldn't pretend. Heck, I couldn't pretend when my feelings for him were new. Guilt was a strong emotion. I understood that better now than I had before, and if that was what he had been feeling all of those months for me, I couldn't blame him for needing to take care of me.

Grabbing my Kindle, I went to the bedroom in my parents' cabin. I was surprised they'd bought a cabin because it didn't seem their type of place, but after staying here, I could definitely understand my dad's reason for loving it. It had a beautiful view of a lake and was so quiet and calm. He probably escaped here for quiet from my mother. That thought made me smile. It had two bedrooms, and I chose the guest room because I didn't want to invade their privacy too much.

Setting my Kindle on the nightstand, I went to the bathroom and ran a bath. The cabin had an amazing bathroom with a huge whirlpool tub. I decided after my first night here that I would work to have this same tub in my house one day. Skylights were positioned over the bathtub, and every night since I got here, I'd taken a bubble bath at night so I could look up and see the stars. It calmed me.

Finishing bathing, I put on my panties and a tank top and hopped into bed with my Kindle. My shoulder was doing well, which surprised me after that day in the alley. I was sure I'd have some setbacks, but after a few days of rest and ibuprofen, it was doing as well as previously. I also continued with the few PT exercises I had been given, and I hoped they were helping to strengthen it. I was doing well. As a matter of fact, all of my bruises from that night had faded. It was almost as if it never happened.

Almost.

I read for a while until I could no longer keep my eyes open, then turned to shut off the lamp and put my Kindle down. I'd learned my first few nights to be tired by keeping my mind occupied right up until I fell asleep. It helped stave off the nightmares by giving me less time before I fell asleep to think. It didn't stop them, but it helped.

And I would take all the help I could get with that.

I had decided earlier today that tomorrow would be the day I'd head back. I was stronger now. At least strong enough to face my brother and Ben. And hopefully strong enough to stick to my guns.

I didn't think I would ever feel strong enough to face Christian.

I wasn't sure when it happened, but I realized at some point over the past two months, I'd fallen in love with him. I thought initially it was because he took care of me when I needed someone the most, and he made me feel special. But as time went on, and I became more honest with myself, I realized my feelings for him had started a lot earlier than that. Maybe from the moment he saved me from being mauled by Jake and Ben and whispered in my ear. I felt special that very first day.

And then I didn't.

My relationship with him had been such a roller coaster of emotions that we couldn't continue like that, but in my heart, I knew if I stayed close to him, I wouldn't be strong. I wouldn't be able to stay away from him. We were magnets with crazy strong chemistry, which made my decision to leave New Hope much easier.

Because it was necessary.

I was warm, warmer than I'd been in almost two months. I snuggled deeper into my covers and sighed at their warmth. There was a faint smell of something spicy that I wanted to get closer to, so I pushed closer until I felt the warmth against my face and the smell, stronger now, hit my nose. What a beautiful dream. To feel this warm and safe, and protected.

"Baby, you need to stay still." I heard in my dream.

It made me smile because it sounded like something Christian would have said to me. I pushed closer to the warmth. Why couldn't I get close enough? I pushed my leg forward until it slipped through a space and pulled myself even closer to the warmth.

"Fuck." I heard groaned. And then arms came around me and pulled me tight into something hard and hot. This might be the most realistic dream I'd ever had. A hand ran up the side of my leg to my hip and over to lay against my ribs. I heard the groan again, but this time, it sounded loud and close to my ear. I shook my head. This seemed too real. My eyes popped open to see nothing but a wall of muscle. I tilted my head back and was met with the most beautiful and familiar blue eyes.

I jumped, trying to move back, but felt his arms tighten around me. "Christian," I whispered. "What are you doing here?"

The room was still dark, and looking at the window, I saw it was dark outside too. I couldn't have been asleep very long. "How did you get in here?" I whispered.

He stared into my eyes and moved his hand up to rest against my cheek. I licked my lips and watched as his eyes shifted down to stare at them.

He slid his body down until we were face-to-face and pushed his nose into my neck. "I missed how you smell." His voice was sultry and low.

He ran his hand down past my hip again and circled around to my back, pushing his hand up under my tank top to lay his hand flat against the skin of my back. "I missed how you feel," he whispered in my ear.

He pulled his face from my neck and lifted to rest his forehead to mine. Lips so close I could feel his breath hit mine. "I missed how you taste."

He pressed his lips to mine, so softly, rubbing them back and forth slowly. Running his tongue along the seam of my lips, I opened them with a moan. He kissed me slow and sweet. He pulled back, both of us breathing heavily, but not putting much distance between us.

"I'm here because I missed you," he whispered. "Because I can't live without you." He ran his lips along mine slowly again. "Because I was so scared of losing you that I left you."

"Christian," I whispered, tears filling my eyes at his beautiful words.

He kissed me again, deeper this time, then pulled back while I tried to pull him forward. How does he do that to me? How could he make me feel so quickly?

He put his forehead back to mine and pulled me as close as I could get. My leg tucked between his and my arms wrapped around his middle, resting on his back. I could feel his erection hard against my thigh. "I'm so sorry, baby," he whispered, running his hand up and down the bare skin of my back. "Please tell me you forgive me. I can't keep going without you."

I pulled my arms forward until I held his face between my hands. "I didn't leave because you weren't there for me," I whispered. "I left because you were. Because you all were. And so many people got hurt. Because of me."

He frowned and shook his head. "Not because of you, baby. Because of him. Everybody who was there for you would do it all over again because they love you."

I shook my head. "I feel so guilty."

He pulled my hands from his face and wrapped them around his back as he rolled us until he was holding himself above me. My leg was still wrapped up in his and his hand had moved from the skin on my back to rest right below my breast, his thumb moving back and forth across the swell at the bottom. Leaning forward, he kissed me again but more passionately and ran his thumb up to run over my nipple. I moaned in his mouth until he shifted to lay between my legs and used both hands to pull my tank up, uncovering my breasts. His tongue swept across my nipple, and I arched my back. He brought his mouth back to mine and used his thumb and forefinger to roll my nipple.

"Christian." I moaned against his lips.

"I want to show you what you mean to me," he whispered against my lips before he kissed me slowly. "And then I'm going to take you home and let everyone else tell you what you mean to them."

I stiffened and shook my head but didn't get to protest too much because he bent down and kissed me again. Not slow this time, but hard. Hard enough that I thought he might have bruised my lips. He used both hands to push my top the rest of the way up and only broke the kiss long enough to pull it over my head. I ran my hands down over the hard muscles of his back, savoring the feel of his warm skin against my hands. Running my hands down until I hit the top of his boxer briefs, I put my hands under the band and pushed down until I could run my hands over the bare skin of his firm butt. I squeezed his cheeks and pulled him hard into me while lifting to rub his cock against the silk of my panties, right where I needed him.

"Fuck, baby." He groaned into my neck. "I'm trying to go slow here, but that's not helping."

"I don't want to go slow," I whispered. "I need you. I need you to make me forget."

He pulled back, looking into my eyes. "Whatever you need. I'll always give you whatever you need."

He crawled down, pulling my panties over my hips and slowly down my legs until he pulled them free and threw them behind him. I closed my eyes when his lips and tongue moved up my legs, slowly kissing their way back to me. When he reached the top of my thighs, he pushed my legs farther apart, and I stiffened. This was so intimate. I wasn't sure if I could be this intimate and keep my resolve. All thoughts of stopping him fled when his tongue slid up the seam of my sex and over my clit. He sucked it into his mouth and ran his fingers down, pushing one into me slowly. I arched my back, and he sucked harder, adding another finger.

"Christian, please."

He pulled back and continued kissing up my body, over my stomach, running his tongue along the cleavage between my breasts. He reached my mouth and kissed me slowly but incredibly deep. I didn't think I would have liked the taste of myself, but mixed with him, I found it erotic. I reached down between us and pushed his boxers down over his hips, with him helping to kick them off. I pushed my hands back between us, and he pushed up to his knees, never breaking our kiss. Running my hands down, I wrapped my hands around his hard cock and felt him push forward into my hand.

He broke the kiss but didn't move his lips from mine. "Touch me," he panted. "Stroke me harder."

I added some pressure to my strokes along his cock, and he groaned louder this time. I circled my hand around the sensitive head and used my thumb to rub the small amount of cum already dripping from him. He was panting against my lips. "Stop, baby. I don't want to come yet," he growled.

I pulled his cock closer to me and arched back, trying to put him where I needed him most. He took the hint and gently pushed my hands from his cock, then lined it up and pushed into me slowly. We both groaned out loud when he was completely inside. He laid his forehead against mine. I wrapped my legs around the back of his thighs and pushed up. He pulled almost completely out and pushed back in slowly. So slowly. His kisses even matched the slow rhythm of his thrusts.

"More, Christian." I groaned. "I need more."

He pulled out and flipped me to my stomach, putting his hands on my hips and pulling them up until he could push back in to me. We both groaned at the new depth he reached, taking me this way. Wrapping his arms around my belly, he pulled me up to my knees with him until my back was to his front. I rolled my head back until it lay against his shoulder. He ran his hands down and over my belly to cup his hand over me, using his thumb to strum my clit while he thrust slowly. I tried to arch my back while he thrust, but this position limited my ability to move, which made it feel more intimate.

"I'm going to come." I panted out.

"Yes, baby. Come for me." He groaned, rubbing my clit faster and thrusting in short, deep strokes while running his hand up to lay his hand over my breast and pull on my nipple. My legs started to shake and tingle while my orgasm came fast and strong, barreling through my body, causing me to arch and cry out.

He quickly bent me forward and pulled out, rolled me to my back and thrust in, prolonging my orgasm. He pushed my knees up toward my chest and started thrusting faster.

"Harder, Christian." I moaned.

"Jesus, I can feel you tightening. Are you coming again?" He groaned on a thrust.

"I don't think I stopped yet." I panted.

His body tightened, and he pushed forward, holding himself deep until I heard, "Fuck, yes," on a groan. He buried his face in my neck while his orgasm coursed through him.

We lay still, him still throbbing deep inside me and my legs still wrapped tight around his legs. He pulled his head from my neck and looked into my eyes.

He started moving again but slower this time. Looking into my eyes, he said the words that were both exhilarating and scary. "I love you, Lucy."

Tears filled my eyes. Shaking my head, I said, "Christian…"

"Stop." He leaned down to kiss me. "I love you. I love you more than anything in my life." He kissed me again, just as softly. "I want to spend the rest of my life showing you how much I love you. And I'm going to keep saying it until you believe me."

"Ti amo e tu e mai vi lascerà nuovamente…" he whispered.

Tears slid from the corners of my eyes, and he wiped them away with his thumbs.

"What did you say?" I whispered.

He smiled a beautiful, blinding smile. "I said, I love you, and I will never leave you again."

He leaned in and kissed me softly. "I promise baby. I promise those words forever."

Chapter Thirty-four

Lucy

I slept like the dead.

After his promise and declaration, I fell asleep and didn't hear anything until I woke up to the smell of coffee and the sounds of food cooking. I looked at the nightstand and saw it was ten in the morning, and the sun was shining through the window. Deciding to get up because we had a lot to talk about, I jumped out of bed, pulled on yoga pants and a shirt from my bag, and headed to the bathroom. I tried while brushing my teeth to come up with a way to start the impending conversation, but I honestly had no idea what he was thinking, so I planned to follow his lead.

Maybe.

Walking into the kitchen, I felt my stomach clench with nerves. He turned as I cleared the doorway and smiled.

"I heard you go into the bathroom," he explained. "Thought you could use this." He motioned to the coffee.

I walked to him and reached out for the cup. "Thanks," I squealed when he suddenly grabbed me and kissed me hard on the mouth.

"Stop thinking," he mumbled against my lips, his hands still holding my hips. "I can practically feel the anxiety pouring off you."

"I'm not that bad," I grumbled, pulling away and heading to the counter to sit on a stool.

"Yes, you are, but most of that is my fault." Chuckling, he brought a plate of eggs and bacon over and set it in front of me. "And I'm going to fix it."

I looked up at the plate in front of me in time to watch him walk back over to the stove. Wearing only pajama pants, he looked amazing. I watched the muscles in his back flex beneath his smooth, tan skin. It was completely unfair to wake up and look that good. He turned and caught me staring, which brought a cocky smirk to his face. I rolled my eyes and picked up my fork, my stomach already rumbling.

He sat across from me at the counter and watched as I took the first bite. "Thank you for making breakfast."

He smiled and started eating from his own plate. "I thought we could use a good meal before we start the drive back today."

I looked back up at him and nodded. "You know I had already planned to head back today," I said.

I watched his eyebrows rise and eyes widen in surprise. "What?"

He shook his head. "Nothing. I just figured you'd put up more of a fight about leaving."

"Nope. I'm ready to go back." I took a sip of my coffee.

Wrapping my hands around the coffee mug, I asked the question I was curious about since he woke me up last night. "So, how long did it take you to guys to find me?"

He grinned and picked up his own cup. "Four days."

"Four days. That's it?" I was actually surprised, considering I thought I'd done better than that.

Taking a drink, I watched his throat move as he swallowed. How in the hell was that sexy too?

"Actually, that pissed Striker off." He set his cup back down. "He said that was three days too many."

I laughed. I could definitely imagine Striker saying that.

"Although he was impressed by you, and I'm guessing not a lot impresses the guy."

I shook my head and frowned. "Why?"

"Well, let's see." He started counting off on his fingers. "You turned off your cell. You got money out of your account before you even left the state so we couldn't track withdrawals or monitor your credit cards. Oh, and my favorite…" He leaned forward. "Writing out your official statement and overnighting it before you left the first place you were staying."

I frowned. "I didn't want Luke to get into any trouble because I didn't go into the police station and do it. I was hoping the way I did it was okay."

He smiled wide. "It was fine. He was actually really proud of you for doing that."

I leaned forward and took another drink when something occurred to me. "Wait, if you knew where I was, why didn't you come here before last night?"

"I've been here the whole six weeks you have, Luce. We found you at the beach house and held off to see your next move, hoping you would come home on your own. But after Luke got the package, we knew you weren't ready, so I followed you here and have been staying at a hotel in town."

I shook my head, confused. "Why? Why would you do that?"

He put his cup down and pulled mine from my hands, setting it on the counter. Grabbing my hand, he held it between his own and rubbed his thumb over my palm. "You asked for time, so I wanted to make sure you got that. But last night I needed to see you, to feel you in my arms. I couldn't stay away any longer."

I stared at him, stunned by his admission. "You put your life on hold for two months." I frowned before whispering, "For me."

"You really don't get this at all, do you?" When I shook my head, he got up from his chair, came around, and pulled me from my chair. Wrapping his arms around my waist, he pulled me close and leaned down. "I love you. I'd do anything for you."

205

This man. This man who had made me feel alone and rejected but also alive and beautiful. I needed to tell him my plans to leave, but standing in front of him, I couldn't. I wanted to experience this time together. I wanted to pretend this could be my future, if only for today. He believed the words he said, and I even thought they were true to some extent, but our time together had been intense and unpredictable, so how sure could he be?

I loved him.

I knew I'd loved him since the moment I met him.

I'd tried to hide it because although I'd like to believe in love at first sight, it always seemed highly unlikely. So far, I'd been impulsive, and that wasn't me. I couldn't trust myself when my feelings for him made me so impulsive.

And I couldn't trust his feelings.

I rose on my tiptoes and wrapped my hand around his neck, pulling him down for a kiss. What started as a simple kiss quickly turned hard and hot, with a clash of tongues fighting for control. Except I didn't want to be in control. I loved that he wanted control. With him, I didn't always have to think. I didn't have to know what came next because he did. He shifted to push me up against the wall. He grabbed my hands and pushed them up and over my head to lay flat against the wall. Yes, I loved that. I loved that I trusted him enough when we are together this way to allow myself to feel this powerless. Leaving one hand to hold my wrists, he used the other wrapped around my waist to pull me closer.

He pulled my arms back down and wrapped his completely around me. He started walking down the hallway as he ran his lips down my neck and then back to my own. Shoving his leg between mine, he kept pushing me backward while his tongue continued to slide alongside mine. I groaned when he moved his hands to round the bottom of my butt and pulled me harder against him.

I broke the kiss but didn't move away. "Where are we going?"

"Time for a shower." He spoke roughly, leaving no room for discussion, but it wasn't like I would say no anyway. "I should've asked last night, but I was too wound up in you." He paused, and I widened my eyes, afraid of what he would say. "But are you on birth control?"

Feeling confused, I shook my head. "Why?"

He leaned in closer. "We didn't use a condom."

Oh, I hadn't even realized that. I don't think I'd ever been that immersed in someone that I stopped thinking. "Yeah, I am. On birth control, I mean."

He nodded slowly. "Okay, but just so you understand, it wouldn't have mattered to me either way. I would've been fine with whatever happened. That's how sure I am of what we are together." He finished with a small bite to my bottom lip, which made me moan.

I grabbed the top band of his pajama pants and started pushing them down while he worked to get my T-shirt up and over my head. We shed our clothes quickly after that, and he leaned in to turn on the shower. I took that time to move behind him and run my hands up the muscled contours of his back. I placed my lips against the back of his shoulder and pressed my body as close as I could get to his. I heard his sharp intake of breath and grinned, loving the feeling of making a man like this want me. Running my hands around and over his flat abs, I let them drift slowly down until I could wrap both of my hands around his hard cock.

He grabbed the shower wall and groaned while I stroked him slowly from root to tip. I physically felt his control snap, and I stiffened. He turned quickly and pulled me into the shower with him, pushing me up against the shower wall, his front to my back. When the water flowed over us, I leaned my head back into him. He ran his hands along my ribs and up over my breasts, pulling on my nipples until I moaned, "Christian, yes. More. I need more."

He ran his hands back to my hips and pulled them, gently pushing my head forward until I could rest my cheek against the tiled shower wall. "I can't go slow this time." He groaned.

"I don't want slow," I said, practically begging him.

All he needed was permission because I immediately felt him line up and slam into me. I hissed and rolled my head so my forehead was pressed to the wall, pushing my ass out. He hadn't been this deep before. I felt so incredibly full as he hit places he hadn't been with his powerful thrusts.

"Come for me, baby," he demanded. "You have me too fucking wound up. I can't last much longer."

His words did as much for me as his long, hard thrusts because with only a few more, I yelled, "Christian, yes. Right there."

As I groaned out my release, he pumped his hips a few more times before he pressed himself to my back against the wet, tiled wall.

When I'd caught my breath, I leaned back a little, settling against his hard body when his arms came around me, and he rested his chin on my shoulder.

"How is it possible that it gets better every time with you?" he asked in a serious voice.

I smiled, because honestly, I felt the same way, but I didn't have much to compare it to. He pushed off and grabbed the shampoo.

"Ready for that shower?" He winked when I turned to face him, making me giggle.

Chapter Thirty-five

Lucy

"We're going to have to build up your stamina." Christian grinned.

We were a little over two hours into our three-hour trip, and I had only woken up about one minute ago. I hadn't realized how tired I was until we were in the car and driving, but I obviously was because Christian said it had only taken about five minutes for me to fall asleep. He teased me about needing rest after our workout, which was fairly accurate, but I wasn't admitting that.

I rolled my eyes. "Maybe you bore me to sleep."

I took a chance and looked over at him only to see the cocky expression on his face. "Yeah, that's it."

Shaking my head, I turned my phone back on and started typing out a text.

"What are you doing?" he asked, curiously.

"Texting Landon that I'm on my way back." I answered, somewhat distracted. "Actually, Ben and Landon."

The air in the car changed, and I glanced over at Christian, whose jaw was clenched and his eyes set on the road.

"What's wrong?" I asked, cautiously.

"Nothing," he snapped.

My eyebrows hit my hairline. "You sure about that?"

"I already told the boys we were heading back. I don't know why Ben needs to be texted separately," he grumbled.

Confused by this, I said, "Well, first, I didn't know you already told them. And second, it's my brother and my best friend. I feel like I owe it to them."

I realized my mistake when I watched his nostrils flare and hands tighten on the wheel.

"It's Ben and me, right?" When he didn't answer, I continued, sad that he couldn't understand. "Christian, I've been friends with Ben for a long time now. That's not going to change. At least not by me. I care about him."

He huffed. "Yeah, I can't exactly forget that when he's always standing between us."

"You're the one putting him there," I whispered.

I'd hoped we would have the rest of the day because this morning had been so amazing, but I realized it wasn't possible. My relationship with Ben had been a problem for Christian from the beginning, and I couldn't change his mind about that. He would always wonder if there was more between us.

"Have you two ever kissed?" he tentatively asked.

I wrinkled my nose. "What? Ewww, no."

The tension that had been monopolizing the conversation dissipated when I heard him laugh.

He began laughing hard enough that I had to ask, "What's so funny?"

He choked on his laughter, and I waited until he was only chuckling for him to answer. "Ewww? Jesus, I can't wait to tell Ben that."

He was right. That was funny, so I found myself laughing too. It was funny because Ben loved his reputation for being irresistible to women, so hearing I thought it would be gross to kiss him would definitely piss him off.

We laughed together, something we had never done, I realized.

All this time together and we'd never just talked or laughed. Nothing about us was normal. My fear was that when the excitement was over, and he saw who I was, he might feel differently.

When he was silent for a few minutes, I decided it was time to talk about my plans. Working up the nerve was the hardest part because I knew he would not be very receptive.

"So, I'm planning to leave New Hope and start somewhere fresh," I stated calmly, proud of myself for being matter-of-fact.

"Oh, yeah?" he answered without the reaction I expected or any reaction at all actually.

"Did you hear what I said, Christian?" I wondered if he was even listening.

He turned his head to glance at me before looking back at the road. "You're planning on moving, right?"

My eyebrows drew together. "Umm, yeah."

"Why?" he asked, calmly.

This was not how I thought he would react, and it was throwing me off. I expected yelling and him making demands. Not disregard.

"I just think it's for the best."

"The best for who? You?"

I swallowed. "Well, of course, for me, but I think for everyone else too."

"Bullshit." He shook his head. "Who are you to decide what's best for everyone? Did anyone ask you to do that?" He continued without waiting for an answer. "You know what I think? I think you're scared. Scared to face everyone who was hurt by that bastard because for some dumb-ass reason, you think they blame you."

"They do blame me." I was angry. He didn't know. He wasn't there.

"Who the fuck told you they blame you?" His voice was low.

Shaking my head, I tried to end the conversation. I didn't want to talk about it anymore. "It doesn't matter."

"Tell me," he growled.

"Christian, it doesn't matter. They have every reason to blame me. I went back to work when I should've stayed home and kept all of this away from them."

"You had a retired officer there with you who was more than qualified to make sure everything went smoothly. You were right. You couldn't hide forever. And everyone is fine now." He glanced my way. "Artie is fine."

I nodded. "I know."

He frowned. "You know? How do you know?"

I sighed. "I called Sam a few weeks ago from the coffee shop in town. One of the waitresses let me use her phone. He told me Artie was awake and had to do physical therapy, but it looked like he hadn't lost the use of anything. Just has some weakness on his right side."

I had been so relieved when I'd heard that, I cried. Right there, like a crazy person in the coffee shop. People stared at me while I thanked the waitress and wandered back out, but I didn't care. I didn't realize how much fear I was holding concerning Artie until I heard he would be okay.

It was quiet for a few minutes, and obviously he was stewing over the fact I'd called Sam and not him for information, but what he didn't know was how often I sat holding my phone, wanting to hear his voice. I almost gave in a few times, but then I'd remember my vow to put distance between us, and I'd put my phone away again.

The rest of the drive was silent, but I should've expected that when I told him about my call to Sam and my text to Ben. Unintentionally, I had made that line between us much more solid.

Arriving home, I felt a mixture of relief and fear. Christian carried in my bag for me, and I thanked him but didn't make a move to do anything else. He watched me curiously as I moved around the apartment until I finally headed into the kitchen to get a drink of water.

"Do you want a drink?" I asked when he followed me.

He shook his head. "You're fucking unbelievable, you know that?

"What?"

Leaning in close to me, he repeated, "I said you're unbelievable."

"I heard you," I snapped. "I just don't know why you said that."

Putting his hands on his hips, he put his head back and closed his eyes. I took this opportunity to walk by him back into the living room to put some space between us.

He followed me. "Running away again, huh?" he asked, sarcastically.

"I'm not running away." I huffed. "I need space."

"Space? How much fucking space do you need? You just had two damn months of it." He paused and moved closer to me. "You've been running since I met you, and I have no fucking clue what will make you stop."

I snapped. "Me?" I yelled. "I'm the one running away?" I leaned forward and tilted my head to the side. "What about you, Christian? How many times have you left? How many times have you run away from me?"

He removed the distance between us in a few long strides and came to stand right in front of me. "I did leave. You're right. But not because I was scared, like you are. I left to save myself from the inevitable."

"Oh, yeah?" I said, sarcastically. "What's that?"

He leaned back and opened his arms wide. "This!" he yelled. "Exactly what we're doing right now. Me trying to figure out how to get in there." He pointed at my chest. "And to sort through all the crazy shit in your head at the same time. But I can't get in there, can I?" He kept yelling, desperately. "You're never going to let me in, are you?"

I didn't answer. I couldn't. I was afraid of what would come out of my mouth if I opened it, so I didn't answer or look at him. I looked at the floor and shook my head. I heard him go to the door, and I heard him pause, maybe waiting for me to stop him, but I didn't do that either.

I didn't do anything.

"I tried, Lucy." His voice sounded pained. "I busted my ass to show you how I feel."

He paused, and I thought he was done, but instead, he left me with a few final words that I knew would stay with me forever. "I can't be the only one fighting. And I'm tired of fighting for something I can't win."

I heard the door open, and I closed my eyes, feeling the tears building behind my eyelids, and with a few parting words, the fight was over. "So you win, Lucy."

I heard the click of the door closing and finally looked up, sobbing outwardly now that I realized I'd just thrown away the best thing in my life.

Chapter Thirty-six

Lucy

It didn't take long for word of my return to get around. My phone was beeping with messages before I even got out of bed the next morning. After Christian had left, I went to my room and cried until I was empty, and exhaustion took over. I fell asleep in my clothes, but not before I sent out a few texts, letting everyone know I was tired and would call them back tomorrow. I was afraid they would come to see me if I didn't, and I couldn't see anyone else tonight.

Getting out of bed, I glanced at my suitcase that I still hadn't unpacked and decided I still didn't feel like it. Instead, I headed to the bathroom. After a long, hot shower, I stood in front of the bathroom mirror and using my towel, wiped off the steam. What I saw looking back at me made me cringe. Swollen eyes that were red and bloodshot called attention to the fact that I had cried for hours and sleep had not erased that. In fact, I didn't think I'd cried in my lifetime the amount I had cried in the past few months.

After dressing, I headed to the kitchen. With the coffee brewing, I returned some texts and called Ben and Landon because I owed them that much. I was lectured by both of them, which I expected and accepted without complaint. The truth was, I had done what I needed to do without much thought for those who cared about me, and that was selfish.

But I still wouldn't have done it differently.

I'd needed time to think, to sort through my feelings and my guilt, alone. To determine what was best for my future. And I had. Or at least I thought I had until Christian showed up. He made me question my choices and feelings, but in the end, I pushed him away just like I knew I would. Some people were meant to be alone.

My thoughts, fortunately, were interrupted by my doorbell. Looking at the clock, I realized it was almost noon, and all I wanted to do was go back to bed. Taking a deep breath, I went to the door and checked the peephole.

Confused, I pulled the door open only to see Brody's brooding face.

"Never took you for a runner." That was his greeting as he pushed through and closed the door behind him.

"Brody, I…" I started but was quickly interrupted.

"We lost manpower for four days because of that. Four days we should've been working other cases, but half our guys were looking for you. And being a small group, that's a big loss." He stood facing me, hands on his hips.

"I watched my brother go crazy for four days." He lowered his voice. "Because of you."

I looked at the floor in guilt.

More guilt.

"He was tearing this fucking town apart to find you." He ran his hands through his hair, angrily. "And if that wasn't enough, we had another brother and your brother"—he paused long enough to point at me and lean in—"breathing down our necks. All for you."

"I'm sorry," I whispered, swallowing hard to control the threat of tears.

"I didn't tell them it wasn't worth it even though I thought it was. I didn't tell them that some people never want to be found because they would never hear that. I told them we would find you and bring you home." He turned away from me, shaking his head. "And not thirty minutes ago, I was sitting in my office when my brother, who by all rights should've been fucking ecstatic today because his girl was finally home, came barreling into the building looking for a fight."

He went to stand and look out the window, down to the street. I stayed quiet because he didn't need or want my excuses.

"And when he finally calmed down, do you know what he told me?" He turned to face me and tilted his head.

I shook my head because I wasn't sure, and I didn't dare guess.

"He told me your plans to run again." His face like granite, he continued. "And I wasn't even fucking surprised."

He brushed past me and walked straight to my door but didn't open it before he turned to face me again. I looked him in the eye, mine full of tears, and waited.

His voice was low and almost sounded pained when he spoke. "I never saw him fight for something or someone the way he has for you. We're a lot alike, you know. And we only fight for something we feel down in our bones." He paused and then dealt his lethal blow. "It's your turn to fight now. For him and for yourself. And if you don't, then you're not the person I thought you were. And you don't deserve him."

I watched him leave without a response. I didn't call him back and try to explain because the truth was, I had no defense. My reasons were starting to blur and feel less, well, reasonable. I turned to get my cup of coffee, but I bypassed the kitchen and went to my bedroom.

I laid down on top of the covers on my bed and for the first time tried to be honest with myself about why I always ran and why I still do. It wasn't always physically leaving either. I was realizing that I had emotionally checked out on people so many times that it made sense why my friendships or relationships had never worked. Except Ben, and that was only because he wouldn't let me. Landon either. Which only further cemented the fact that Ben's and my relationship was always supposed to be exactly what it was. Platonic. I would never run from him because he didn't cause enough emotion in me to be scared.

Like Christian had and still did.

The doorbell once again rang, interrupting my thoughts, and I strongly considered not answering it for fear it was someone else coming to yell at me. Assuming they wouldn't leave until I let them in, I got up and padded down the hall once again to answer the door. I didn't even check the peephole before I braced and opened the door. Standing before me was the last person I ever expected to see.

I swung the door open and stared.

"Hello, Lucy," she said in her soft voice.

"Hi," I croaked out.

She smiled. "I don't think I ever introduced myself, but I'm Lorraine, Artie's wife."

I nodded but was in shock she was standing at my door.

"I'd like to talk to you for a few minutes if I could come in?" she asked quietly.

That shook me out of my stupor, and I stood to the side, motioning for her to come in.

Some sense came back to me. "Would you like something to drink?"

She smiled sweetly. "No thank you, dear. I'm fine." She sat down on my couch and clutched her purse in her lap.

"I wanted to talk to you about Artie," she said.

I slowly sat across from her in the chair. "Okay."

She took a deep breath, and I watched as her eyes filled with tears. Oh god, this was going to be bad, and I wasn't sure I could take another blow today.

"The day that you came to see Artie in the hospital had been a particularly bad day, seeing as he hadn't woken up yet. This was a worry for everyone, including the doctors. I was in a bad place and mourning what I thought was going to be the loss of my soul mate."

She took a tissue out of her purse and wiped her eyes. My heart broke for her as she continued.

"What I need to tell you, what you need to really hear is that I don't blame you for any of this, and neither does Artie." She pulled another tissue out of her purse and handed it to me. I smiled a wobbly smile to thank her.

"The truth is, this could have happened at any time in our lives, considering his job and also who he is as a person. I had prepared every day for that news when he was on the force, but once he retired, I'd let that fear go. I'd let those fears run my life for a very long time, and it was unfair of me to take that out on you." She paused to wipe her eyes, and I waited anxiously for what else she could possibly have to say.

I was so glad I waited.

"Both Artie and I were blessed that awful day. I finally let all the fear go because my worst fears were recognized, and we survived it. Artie finally admitted life is too short to be in danger for all of it and has officially retired. Again." She laughed at that in a soft way. "Sounds crazy, believe me, I know. But we became an even stronger team having faced that fear together."

I swallowed hard. "I don't know what to say,"

She stood then, and I followed. "There's nothing to say except that I'm sorry for how I treated you that day, especially when you didn't deserve it." She started walking to the door but then paused and turned back to me. "Facing your fears is an incredibly freeing experience. I know that now. And if you learn nothing else from this horrible time, remember that. Remember that fear is only an emotion and one that can be controlled."

"How?" I whispered, desperate for someone to give me the answer.

She leaned in to give me a hug, which I returned, and held on tightly.

Pulling back, she put both of her hands on my shoulders. "Face it," she urged me softly. "Head-on, face the one thing you're most afraid of. I'll bet when you do, you'll feel more alive than you've ever felt."

I nodded and leaned in for another hug. "Thank you," I whispered.

She smiled, sweetly. "Now promise me you'll come visit us. Artie's been itching to see you and make sure you're all right."

"I promise. I will soon."

We said our goodbyes at the door again, and I closed it only long enough to grab my purse and keys and run to my car.

Chapter Thirty-seven

Lucy

"I'm sorry, Lucy. He's not here." An immediate feeling of rejection overwhelmed me.

When I closed the door to Lorraine, I opened the new door she'd shown me. Now I was standing in the front lobby of Christian's offices and staring into Jax's solemn face.

"Do you know where he is?" I asked anxiously.

He shook his head. "No, sorry. He just took off. You could try his place."

I realized then that I had no idea where he lived. I had never been to his house. I asked Jax for his address, and he hesitantly gave it to me.

I understood why.

I drove to his house, a small log home complete with a rustic-looking fence and a barn. I thought it very fitting for Christian. He wasn't there. I knocked even though I didn't see his truck in the driveway, but there was no answer, and he didn't seem to be around the barn. Despondent, I sat in my car for a few minutes in his driveway, trying to decide what to do next.

Maybe this was for the best. I should have taken some time to think about my plan and even what I wanted to say. I wasn't sure I was strong enough to give him everything he wanted. Thinking back, I could see all that he had been doing for me. How he was slowly and patiently teaching me to trust him, to rely on him. Without my mind clouded by fear and guilt, I could finally see how he had taken care of me when I was hurt. He'd held me when I was scared and battling nightmares, trying to seem brave, but knowing deep down that I wasn't. I was hiding. Hiding from him. Hiding from friends and even my family. I was using my past as a compass for my future, but because of that, I was completely ruining any chance I had for a happy future. Beyond all of that, I was hiding from myself so I couldn't be rejected or alone but ended up being both.

But I wasn't alone. I hadn't been rejected. Christian had done everything he could to convince me that he was with me all the way. He refused to leave me alone. He'd never really rejected me, at least not because of me. He was always trying to protect me and his family by denying what he wanted. I'd just never trusted that what he wanted was me. But I could trust him. I could trust what he'd said because he'd always followed it up with his actions. What I couldn't trust was myself. I couldn't trust my ability to make good decisions, so I'd hidden from people and experiences and especially from life. But I couldn't hide from Christian. He never gave up on me, even when I was at my lowest with guilt consuming me. Instead, he kept pushing in closer while I pushed him away. Up until yesterday, he still hadn't given up on me. He'd still been doing everything he could to make me feel safe and loved and protected. I never did any of that for him.

"It's your turn to fight now." Brody's voice said in my head.

He was right. It was my turn to fight for something and someone who had scared the hell out of me.

"Face the one thing you're most afraid of. You'll feel more alive than you've ever felt." Lorraine's voice echoed in my head.

With a newfound determination, I knew what I wanted to say and what I needed to admit if I ever wanted to move forward.

Feeling a riot of nerves in my belly, I backed out of the driveway and started driving. I drove to all of the places he liked to eat with no luck. Next, I tried Jax's house because I knew where that was, but again no luck. I drove around for hours, looking for his truck, but after a while, I started to feel it was hopeless and contemplated going home. Looking at the time on the clock on my dash, I saw it was almost six.

Dinnertime.

There was one place that always had dinner ready and their doors open, so I turned the car and headed in that direction. I couldn't believe I hadn't thought of it before.

Parking my car on the side of the road, I picked out his truck easily. It was hard to miss. He hadn't had it when he came for me yesterday. Instead, he had the boys pick it up after he got to the cabin so he could ride home with me. Just the fact he'd thought of that reminded me why I was doing this. And that they did that for him, reminded me of all the love this family had to share.

And they'd shared it, without any hesitation, and with so many, but especially with someone who hadn't always deserved it.

I anxiously approached and was surprised when the door opened before I even arrived.

"Lucy?" The smile that greeted me, while being pulled into a hug, transformed my nerves into something else. Something beautiful.

I walked into the one place where I felt loved. Where I'd felt acceptance from the first time I sat at the table. The place where all my fears stopped following me.

The place where it all began.

The place that felt like home.

"Look who's here!" I watched as what felt like a million sets of eyes turned to me, but I was only looking for one. And I found those blue eyes that I had gotten so caught up in that first day here, in this house. He was sitting by his dad and across from Ben. My own brother by his side made my heart swell; they had also

223

welcomed him into their amazing family. Jax, looking past me to Kasey who was still standing beside me and smiling knowingly.

Anna rushed around the table and hugged me. With tears in her eyes, she whispered, "We're so happy you're back."

"Welcome home, darlin'," Jack boomed, then followed with a long, hard hug. I hugged him back just as hard, secretly wishing I had this with my dad. He leaned his head down close to my ear and spoke quietly. "I said it before, and I'll say it again. You're good for him."

I pulled back and looked up at him curiously, remembering that conversation in his backyard when we were both hiding. Ignoring the small amount of chatter behind us, I responded, "Yes, but that time you were talking about Ben."

Smiling wide, he leaned in close so I could hear him whisper, "I was never talking about Ben, sweetheart." Patting my cheek, he turned and walked back to his seat.

My eyes widened in disbelief as I stared at his retreating back. He had known.

Ben, never one to be left out, stood and hugged me, only to say what only Ben would say. "I knew you couldn't stay away too long. Hell, I know I would've missed me if I was you." He winked, to which he earned an eye roll from me, but I smiled even wider.

Looking at Landon, standing next to Ben, I found the support only he could give because he'd made it clear that he knew what I was feeling. I watched him closely when he eventually nodded and smiled.

After wrapping his arms around me for a long hug, he pulled back. "Welcome home."

"You say that like it's our home," I said cautiously, and he waited patiently while I worked up the nerve to ask what I'd wanted to ask since he arrived months ago. "Does that mean you're staying?"

He shrugged. "Yeah, I guess. There are some pretty hot women in this town." I grinned and slapped his shoulder. "Hey! What?

You know that's my only stipulation for moving to a new place." Grinning, he rubbed his shoulder.

"Now I finally see what you and Ben have in common." I spoke to his back as he headed to his seat at the table. I didn't follow him to a seat. Instead, I stayed where I was, facing a table full of people I loved.

"Come sit, Lucy." Kasey pulled out an empty chair beside her, but I shook my head.

With everyone sitting again and all eyes on me, I should've felt nervous, but I didn't. I felt lighter. I felt happy. "I was hoping I could talk to all of you for a minute."

"Of course, Lucy." Anna waved her hand around. "Go ahead, we're listening."

I glanced at Christian who seemed to be having a silent conversation with Jack and froze for a moment, knowing he thought I was here to say goodbye.

I cleared my throat, telling myself not to cry. Taking a deep breath, I said what I should've said a while ago. "I hide. You probably already knew this about me, but I've just figured it out." I listened to everyone chuckle and knew it was true.

Not able to make eye contact with anyone, I looked down at my hands that I was wringing together. "I hid behind Landon while we were growing up." Looking up at Landon, I watched his eyes soften, and I shrugged. "I was shy and awkward, but you let me be that and still made me feel accepted and safe. Though, I never really tried to make any other friends. I only needed you."

I glanced at Ben, who had turned completely in his seat to watch me. "I hid behind Ben to avoid any other relationships." Smiling sadly, I continued, "I never felt confident until you became a part of my life, and I love that you gave me that, but ours became the only relationship I needed. I was able to avoid all others because you gave me everything I needed, and the parts you didn't, I convinced myself I didn't want.

"I hid behind something violent and tried to make myself invisible."

I paused and took another deep breath, glancing at Brody and Jax, sitting side by side, whose expressions turned to granite when I mentioned the assault. "I let that moment in my life become the only thing to drive all of my choices, including who I wanted to be."

Looking back down at my hands, which I still had clasped tightly together, I continued, "I ran away convinced that being alone was the only way to find myself. But I realized after coming back that I was still just hiding."

I finally found the nerve to look at Christian again. He was watching me with so much love in his eyes that I couldn't even imagine how I'd missed it before. "You scare me." I heard a sniffle from somewhere in the room. "I've been hiding from you for a while now, and I've decided to stop. I've discovered that my greatest fear is losing you, not loving you."

I took another deep breath and held up my hand when he stood and started toward me. "Stop, please. I have to do this because I'm scared to, especially in front of people who matter so much to me." He stopped but stayed close. With a small smile, I silently thanked him.

"Today, I had someone very important tell me that facing my fears would set me free. Would make me feel more alive than I had ever felt." Suddenly, the tears I'd been holding back began to break free one at a time. "I want that," I whispered. "I want to feel free. I want to feel safe and loved."

I faced Christian. "You give me that. You make me feel all of that."

I took another deep breath. "I had another person, who quite honestly scares the shit out of me sometimes"—I heard chuckling again and looked at Brody who grinned and winked at me—"but who I've also come to love and respect, tell me it was my turn to fight." I turned my attention back to Christian. "So that's what I'm doing right now. I'm fighting for you, Christian, for me," I whispered, "for us."

Not sure what else to say and emotionally drained, I closed my eyes and dropped my head.

"Can I come to you now?" I heard the low voice I loved so much.

I nodded, not looking up until his arms surrounded me. Burying my face in his neck, I inhaled his comforting scent. "I'm sorry. I'm sorry I'm such a mess," I whispered.

"You're not a mess, baby." he said, softly. "And if you are, then I must love messes."

I smiled and looked up to see him smiling back.

"Say it," he demanded, softly.

"Say what?" I whispered.

"Say what you're still afraid to say." He leaned in close to me, putting his hands on my cheeks. "I promise I'm not going anywhere."

Looking in his eyes, I saw the truth. The truth that had always been there, but we both fought against so hard until we broke. "I love you," I said confidently.

He smiled the biggest smile I had ever seen, and it lit his face in such a way that I knew I would do everything I could in this life to put it there again and often.

I'd been living in the shadows because the fear of rejection had put me there. Today was the first day I stepped out.

And I finally felt free.

Epilogue

Lucy

"It's a boy!" Cheers erupted in a waiting room full of Dimarcos.

I smiled at the proud daddy of this new baby boy, waiting my turn in line to hug him. It had been a stressful nine months for Jake, and I wasn't sure sometimes if he was happy or not, but seeing him now, there wasn't a doubt in my mind.

He was beaming.

"Can we see him?" I heard behind me when I finally had my opportunity to get that hug.

"What's his name?" someone yelled, and I do mean yelled, across the room. I'd been waiting for all of us to be kicked out. Most of us had been here through the night waiting. Jake had called, and it seemed he needed the backing of his family here with him, so we all got up, dressed, and down to the hospital as quickly as possible, except for Kasey who stayed home with a sleeping Mia.

Jax smiled as he spoke into the cell phone at his ear and knew Kasey was celebrating with him via phone.

"Congratulations, Daddy." I leaned back to look up at his face and smiled.

"Thanks, Luce. I can't believe how small he is." Shaking his head in disbelief, he let me go. "I'm going to be the best dad, you know." He smirked.

I laughed. "Of course you are. You don't know any different," I replied, surprised he remembered that conversation from so long ago.

Arms wrap around me from behind, and I leaned back into the safest place I'd ever been. It had only been a month, but Christian and I had been working through the glitches in our relationship that had held us back before. He spent some time talking to Ben, and it seemed he had finally accepted our relationship for what it had always been. A very good friendship.

I, on the other hand, decided it was time to see a therapist to deal with both assaults instead of hiding behind them. Until seeing her, I'd had no idea how much that first assault had affected my life. How much I had buried or how crippling my fear had really become. We'd discovered together that a lot of my fears were because of trust. The fear of putting myself into someone else's hands and trusting them to take care of me. That was something new to me and something I vowed to work on until I learned what other people seemed to already know.

"Boy, are you ever gonna tell us his name?" I laughed because sometimes Jack's Southern roots came out to play and this was one of them. Add in the Italian, and it was anyone's guess what you'd hear. I hadn't known until recently that he had actually been raised in Dallas and only moved to New Hope after he met Anna. That was a story I would love to hear some day.

Looking up at Jake, he smiled even brighter. "Braydon Jackson Dimarco."

Christian's arms tighten and glanced back to see Jack and Jax stiffen before smiling big. I watched as Jax smiled and started talking and I knew he was telling Kasey by the look of pride on his face.

Jack walked over to Jake and grabbed his shoulder. "That's a good name, son," he said sincerely. Then he leaned closer, and I was sure only Jake, Christian, and I could hear him when he asked, "How the hell did you talk her into that?"

Jake smirked. "She was asleep when I filled out the papers." He winked at me. The boom of Jack's laughter felt like it shook the walls in the waiting room, and Christian's body shook behind me with the laughter he was obviously trying to contain.

The crowd dispersed a little after that and we promised to come back later to meet Braydon but wanted to give the new grandparents time with Jake and their grandson. I had yet to see any family of Julie's, and I didn't ask Jake but made a mental note to ask Christian about that later.

The ride down in the elevator was quiet. I think we were both enjoying the thought of a new family member and all that would bring. Walking through the front doors of the hospital, hand in hand, Christian spotted Luke on the sidewalk. I had noticed that he'd left the waiting room almost immediately after Jake made the announcement but was too wrapped up in the excitement to think much about it.

"Luke!" Christian yelled out. I watched Luke turn to us and saw his face pale before I heard Christian's quick inhale. I looked around him to see what made him stop so suddenly and felt all the air leave my lungs.

"What the fuck?" he whispered, voice trembling, watching the figure run to the other side of the street.

"Christian, is that...?" I stopped when he took off running, chasing down the one thing that was still missing from his life.

"Cam!" he roared.

About the Author

Jennifer Hanks is a new and upcoming author of Romance novels, focusing on family, love and laughter. Her love of reading and books in general started at a very young age and has steadily grown into a love of writing as well. She admits to being addicted to all things romance and has no plans of quitting her habit. Jennifer lives in Pennsylvania with her husband and two children. When she's not reading or writing, she can be found with her kids at their various activities. Her house is frequently filled with any combination of her children's friends, nieces, nephews and a variety of pets.

JENNIFER CAN BE FOUND ONLINE AT:

authorjenniferhanks@gmail.com

www.facebook.com/**Jennifer-Hanks**-947981351951214

www.twitter.com/authorjhanks

Made in the USA
Las Vegas, NV
17 June 2021